WELCOME TO ST MILDRED'S & OTHER SHORT STORIES

THE ISLE OF WESBERREY SERIES

STEVEN HIGGS
PENELOPE CRESS

WELCOME TO ST MILDRED'S

A Jessamy Ward Mystery

The Isle of Wesberrey Series

A Short Story

WELCOME TO ST MILDRED'S

"There is much fear here. I sense hopelessness. Loss." Muriel chanted.

Everyone, including me, wanted to know more. "Can you see anything? Can you hear them?"

"She cannot speak. They will discover her," Muriel whispered.

"Who? Who are they?" I wanted to look. Check what our guide was doing. Despite the theatrics, this was a scientific investigation. I cracked open my left eye.

Muriel twisted her neck. Her arthritic bones crunched in response. "The Hellhounds! We are undone!" The shrill cry sliced through the frosty night, stealing our icy breath. A foul stench like rotting eggs filled the void, causing the group to cough and splutter. The sound of snarling dogs encircled us.

Fear trumped curiosity. I screwed my eyes shut and gasped for air. At least my colleagues were with me, our fingers weaved together.

Crashing furniture and clanking pewter echoed throughout the room.

Rabid bites snatched at our legs.

Sweaty palms loosened their grip.

I must not break the circle. I squeezed Ruben's hand beside me. Lekeisha tightened hers on my right.

Wood creaked. The dull shuffle of chair legs and wretched breaths came from the direction of Muriel's chair. My conscience told me to break the chain and help. The poor old woman was imprisoned with cable ties. This was barbaric! But I dared not open my eyes.

They can't hurt me. A vice-like force pressed down on my throat. *They can't hurt us.*

Muriel choked.

Silence.

"YOU MAY OPEN YOUR EYES, my dears. The danger has passed. For now."

The rancid scent of sulphur lingered, the only testament to what we had just witnessed, other than the quivering wrecks finding comfort in their neighbours or alternate type of spirits.

A silver flask was offered and accepted.

Muriel sat withered in her chair. Ties in place. Her hood had fallen back to reveal a frail, pearlescent face. It was hard to imagine this old lady could put on such a show without assistance.

Our job was to find out how they did it.

The head of the psychic association fussed around the

medium, cutting her restraints and helping her into the lounge.

As they walked past us, Muriel paused, steadying herself on my shoulder..

"It isn't over yet, my dears. You will find here the proof you seek. Tonight, lives will be changed forever."

MYSTIC MURIEL, velvet-cloaked medium and spirit wrangler, was our guide for the night in this quaint two-bed cottage, created from the remnants of a convent and allegedly home to the ghost of a young nun.

Rumour has it that she was killed by Thomas Cromwell's agents during a raid in 1532, as part of Henry VIII's dissolution of the monasteries. Residents had long told tales of a dark figure running through the house, sounds of angry dogs, unpleasant odours and physical attacks resulting in bite marks and scratches on their necks, arms, and legs.

Locals warn their daughters to not go near the house after midnight or the hounds would take them too.

Such nonsense is irresistible.

Normally we are wrapped in white lab coats conducting parapsychology research at the local university, but every so often our fearless trio would venture out into the field. Tonight we had joined up with a local ghost-hunting group, the 'Spirit Sleuths' (or as we called them the Scooby-Don'ts) and the Stourchester Psychic Society to explore claims of supernatural activity on the site of the medieval convent of St. Mildred's in Oysterhaven.

The three different investigating groups didn't mix well. While members of the psychic society comforted an exhausted Muriel in the cosy lounge at the front of the cottage, the three of us gathered around the kitchen table. The Scooby-Don'ts checked on their equipment in the bedrooms and hallway upstairs. These breaks were always awkward, like sitting in a darkened theatre waiting for the blackout to end between scene changes in a bad amateur production. No one wanted to talk. Everyone was desperate to get up and leave. Yet we had all committed to remaining till the bitter end.

"My, my! That was some extra spicy juju earlier!" Lakeisha threw her coffee dregs in the sink. "I swear, this time I believed we were all going to die!"

"Do you think she did? The nun, I mean." I massaged my neck.

"Well, eventually," sneered Ruben. "If the *Hounds* didn't get her, then the noose or old age did. Legend says she was a witch. That she steals away young maidens to serve her satanic lord. What utter rot!"

Ruben's comments were unhelpful. He knew what I meant. Ruben had a compulsion for snarkiness that riled me. Words were his weapon of choice.

He was a handsome nerd. Lakeisha liked him, really *liked* him, though she would never admit it. Sometimes though, I felt like I was 'that friend', the one tagging along with her best mate to watch over her, only to be unceremoniously dumped the moment they finally kiss.

To be honest, I am not sure Lakeisha would ride shotgun for me. We were united as long as we sought the same thing, and tonight that was the desire to debunk Mystic Muriel.

Lakeisha flopped down beside me at the waxed oak table.

"Remind me again why we're here with these loonies?" she asked. "I mean, that was quite the display, Oscar-winning. But we could be down the club, girl! I'm getting so horny even Ruben is looking good!"

Ruben's eyebrows arched over the top of his iPad. "I'm in the room, you know."

"Aren't either of you intrigued by what just happened?" I switched on my phone's camera to check my neck for red marks. That was about all I could use it for. The signal was terrible.

"Tabs, I'm more interested in debunking that fraud." Lekeisha's special interest was in anomalistic psychology, or rather the study of how susceptible people are to wanting to believe in an afterlife. "It was very convincing, though. I'd like to know how she simulated the dogs. I swear I could feel their fiery breath around my ankles."

"And I felt hands on my throat too." I leaned over to show her the photo I had just caught on my phone. *How millennial!* I could have shown her my actual neck.

Ruben dismissed our experiences with a deflective wave. "I suspect it was a psychosomatic response to the auditory stimulus. And the fiery breath? Turn up the heating; throw in a few stink bombs." Ruben put down his tablet and wiped his glasses on the sleeve of his checked flannel shirt. "I need to examine the room for speakers."

"The Scooby-Don'ts did a sweep beforehand. They found nothing." I said.

"Tabitha, really? Those anoraks can barely find their way

out of their Mums' basements." Ruben stretched back in his chair and yawned. "Ouija board up next. Should be fun."

~

E.L.I.Z.A.B.E.T.H.

"Elizabeth!" *Could she have a longer name?* My fingers had stiffened into claws on the planchette. The heart-shaped piece of wood was the size of my hand. With so many of us competing for space, it was difficult to maintain just the right touch to ensure a neutral force. Lakeisha's inch long nails didn't help. So far we had found out that someone was there. She meant us no harm. She wasn't alone. And her name was Elizabeth.

"Ask Elizabeth who else is here," several of the psychic society members badgered, *almost* in unison, creating an eerie echo to their question.

With a nod to her enraptured audience, Muriel, huddled and hooded, continued her psychic interrogation. "Thank you, Elizabeth," she sang, "who is here with you?"

The planchette glided across the board spelling out the letters. L.U.C...

"Lucy?" One of the Scooby-Don'ts grew excited, "That's my cat's name!"

The table shook, and the board flew across the kitchen. Cupboard doors rattled and crockery clinked. The room again vibrated to a gnarling, slobbering cacophony.

Muriel cried, "The Hounds are back!"

This time our eyes were open. This time we could see the

rabid canine shapes moving around us in the flickering candlelight.

"I guess they don't like cats!" Ruben quipped.

"Not the time for jokes!" I yelled across the room.

The circle broke up. Groups formed around the table. Some holding hands and praying, others closing their eyes and pulling their companions close. I grabbed Lekeisha's arm for support.

Ruben stood and marched to the overhead cabinet where we had earlier removed mugs for tea and coffee. "My money is on a hidden speaker," he announced, pulling at the handles. "And a projector." The doors resisted him. An unseen force tugged back. "Someone must have super-glued the cupboard door shut!"

Growling shadows darted across the walls and ceiling as behind us, metal pounded against cracking wood, like an axe splintering an oak door.

"They're here! They're here!" Muriel gave out a final anguished cry before slumping into her chair.

"Is she dead?" asked one of the Scooby-Don'ts to a psychic society veteran waving smelling salts under Muriel's nose. *Someone had come prepared.* Could these salts be the source of the sulphur smell?

"Just fainted," the ammonia peddler replied. *How could he tell?* All I could see was a hunched pile of midnight-blue velvet.

The noises stopped. There was no more shattering wood, no more banging. No more dogs. The cupboard door flew open in Ruben's hands. *Not superglue, then...* A departing breeze blew out the candles.

"Quick! Put on the light!" Lakeisha dashed across the

9

kitchen and hit the switch on the wall. The glaring white strip light exposed our shaken party.

"Will Muriel be okay?" I asked. "Should we call a doctor?"

Such exertions couldn't be good for someone of her age. My concern reduced when, seconds later, Muriel's hooded head emerged from the folds of velvet. She appeared restored. Younger even. There was a dewy glow to her cheeks, but maybe that was from perspiration and the glow of the artificial light. She blinked. "Thou art safe now," she said. Muriel's voice sounded strange. I couldn't place how it was different, may have been the ringing in my ears.

THE COMMON PRACTICE at the end of these vigils was for the three of us to head to the local pub to dissect the evening's events if it wasn't an overnight stay. Though often we would pop out for a different encounter with spirits, even if it was. The nearby hostelry was famous for a local brewed ale I was keen to sample. Most nights we sought these delights alone. An evening of forced conversation with the two other groups was unappealing. Out in the night air, though, I felt a strange compulsion to invite Muriel to join us.

"Tabitha, are you crazy?" Lakeisha pulled me aside. "No one wants Mary Berry tagging along."

"I thought you wanted to prove her a fraud," I whispered. "What better way to unmask her than to get her drunk and spill the beans, eh?"

"But she's a hundred and four! Talk about cramping my

..." A purple cable-knit scarf smothered the end of Lakeisha's sentence as she wrapped it across her mouth.

The rest of the psychic society looked on, as confused as Lakeisha was by my invitation. However, Muriel nodded her agreement and bowed her goodbye to her friends.

Both groups left the Scooby-Don'ts behind to clear down their equipment.

The evening had taken its toll. Even the gravel beneath our feet groaned.

We maintained a steady pace as we walked to the Dog and Duck public house, debating between ourselves how it had been done. Muriel, silent, tagged along.

Ruben pushed through the polished wood door, the smooth toffee taste of the local amber nectar already on his tongue. Lakeisha followed close behind, calling out to make hers a double. I was just as keen to get in before they rang the bell for last orders, but Muriel was dithering in the doorway.

I edged around her. "C'mon, we'll just have time to get in one more round!"

She turned away. "I can't go in there. It's an alehouse!"

"Of course it is! And it's almost closing." Feeling a desperate thirst brewing, I left my guest to follow on behind. Maybe it was rude of me to abandon an old age pensioner on the threshold, but it had been a long night and I needed some liquid fortification. Muriel could fend for herself. She was old enough to be my grandmother and was a darn sight more agile than my actual grandma. In fact, she had kept pace with us without so much as a whimper, which made her sudden reticence a tad frustrating.

My order placed, I scanned the bar. The guilt grew louder.

Muriel had had a traumatic evening. Perhaps this was a case of sensory overload or pure burnout. That would confuse anyone. I had been rude and selfish. If my mother was here to witness this behaviour, she would have taken me aside for a stern word or twenty. Ignoring my friends' advice to let her be, I ventured back out into the cold air.

Muriel hadn't gone far. She was curled up on a green painted bench across the road; her cloak wrapped around her knees like a blanket. *Multi-functional velvet, very bohemian.* I sat beside her.

Her shoulders shuddered.

"Muriel, I'm so sorry. Are you okay?"

"Where am I?" she asked.

"At the Dog and Duck, and it's much warmer inside." I stood, tapping her on her raised leg. "Look, if you don't drink, I am sure we can get you a water, or a coke?"

"A coke? What is that?"

"Coca-Cola? Pepsi?"

Muriel's head dropped. "Please, can ye take me back to the convent? Mother Abbess cannot find me here. T'was great folly to leave. The devil was in my thoughts."

"Mother Abbess?" *Good one, Muriel.* She had to be pulling my leg. "C'mon, there's no need for any more theatrics. Your act was very convincing earlier, but there really is no point in continuing. Let's have a little something to round off the evening and go our separate ways, eh?"

"Mistress, prithee, I entreat thee. Thou showest great Christian kindness to thy companions. But associating with a Moor and a Jew? Venturing out after dark? I am sure that our Lord lives within thy heart and I sense thou art a goodly person, despite thy strange attire. Forsooth, I do not wish to judge thee, however, I cannot enter a tavern."

Mistress? A Moor and a Jew? "Seriously, Muriel, enough is enough. Do you want me to buy you a round, is that it?"

The moon gleamed through a gap in the clouded sky, and the shaft of extra light revealed a frightened young woman on the bench beside me. "I am sorry, but who is this Muriel of whom thou speaketh?"

I hesitated. I wanted to say you are, but she wasn't. Not any more. *Think, Tabs, think, how could an old woman have swung her legs up on the seat like this?* This was a simple magician's trick. The good old switcheroo. Somehow Muriel had swapped with a young woman in the dark, back in the cottage, and we hadn't noticed. The shadows, the sounds, all a ploy to distract us. Smoke and mirrors. Velvet cloaks! No cable ties for the Ouija board session, of course. Whoever this was on the bench with me, she was a brilliant actress. Why had they gone to these lengths to fool us? I played along, curious to see where they wanted this charade to go.

"Sorry, I meant... *Elizabeth.* Right? You are Sister Elizabeth?"

'Elizabeth' nodded.

"Well, *Sister*, I will take you back to the convent, but first come inside and warm up. I need you to allow me to finish my pint. Okay? I promise you will come to no harm. Please, take my hand." Elizabeth recoiled from my touch. "Look, if you're worried about the Abbess, I doubt she's hanging out in a tavern after vespers."

The seductive ambience of pub life wafted from across the street. Excited chatter, muted jukebox and stale beer. Pure heaven. "Tabs, get in here, your head's almost flat!" Lakeisha, wedged in the half-open doorway, called across, beckoning me back inside.

"Keish, come here. Sister *Eliz-a-beth* is worried the *Abbess* will see her."

"Sister Elizabeth? Girl, have you been at the cooking sherry? 'Cos, I know your lips haven't touched that pint." Lakeisha tiptoed across the street, hugging herself against the cold air. "Shit! What'd you do with old Muriel?"

"I believe she's back at the cottage." I hoped my friend would understand my pantomime wink and exaggerated tilt of the head. "I have promised *Sister Elizabeth* here that we will help her back *to* the *convent* after our drinks."

Lakeisha knotted her pencil-lined eyebrows. "Oh, *to-the-convent*! Of course. But hey Sis, let's warm you up first. They have a log fire inside."

ONE HAD to admire Elizabeth's commitment to her character. From her on-pointe repulsion at the sight of the local teenage girls in figure-hugging leather and low-cut blouses to her near-hysterical reaction to the flashing slot machine by our table, she had this sixteenth-century nun act down pat.

Drinks downed, Ruben pulled out his smartphone to order us a taxi.

Elizabeth pulled up her hood and started to mutter to herself in Latin.

"Pater noster, qui es in caelis, sanctificetur nomen tuum.
Adveniat regnum tuum.

Fiat voluntas tua, sicut in caelo et in terra."

"What's the witch saying now? Ruben stood up and walked to the bar.

"She's not a witch, she's supposed to be a nun."

Lakeisha rushed to stand by her man. "Potato, potaato. Didn't they execute nuns as witches back then? Like that famous one. She's being her right? The Nun of Kent."

"Elizabeth Barton? Now that's a thought." I turned to our guest. "Are you supposed to be the Mad Maid of Kent? That's brilliant!"

"Et ne nos inducas in tentationem, sed libera nos a malo. Amen."

Ruben was not amused. "How do we know she's not denouncing me as the devil?"

"Calm down. I'm sure it's the Lord's Prayer."

"Ah, well that's alright then." He sneered.

OYSTERHAVEN HAS a wonderful retro-themed taxi company that uses old decommissioned London black cabs that are no longer fit for work in the city. Maybe our young actress had never seen an original Austin FX4 before, but Elizabeth greeted the black devil's carriage with an exorcising round of fretful incantations. Whoever was behind this charade was getting their money's worth.

Both Ruben and Lakeisha raced to pull down the rear-facing seats in front of the cab. I guided our new friend to the back. Once coaxed inside, her laboured prayers steamed up the windows. I tried to calm her down.

"We are heading back to St. Mildred's now. Please try to relax, I'm worried you will hyperventilate."

Elizabeth eyed me with suspicion. At least she ventured to look at me. Whenever Lakeisha or Ruben tried to talk to her, she would flinch and cast her face downwards.

"Tabs, will you quit humouring her!" Lakeisha waved her acrylic talons at me. "This silly little charade is borderline offensive now, you know!" She was right. As a cloistered nun from Tudor times, it was insightful to portray this ignorant fear of my companions, but I could understand why Lakeisha and Ruben were unamused by Elizabeth's authenticity. The entire act was wearing a little thin.

The taxi took a few minutes to reach our destination. Darkness cloaked the cottage and the surrounding buildings, the only source of light was the full moon overhead. We left Ruben to settle with the driver. Elizabeth's spirit seemed to lift as we walked down the gravel path. I imagined she too was growing weary of keeping up the pretence.

Lekeisha rattled the doorknob. "They locked it! Seriously?" She picked up the cast iron knocker, rat-a-tat-tat. "Someone has to be inside! It's maybe just stiff…" She stepped back a few paces and hurled herself towards the door, rebounding off it with equal force.

"Here, let me try." Ruben pushed us aside. "By the way, you all owe me a fiver. The driver charged us double-time. It's just gone midnight! The bast-" He ran towards the door. The wood creaked in the frame but refused to budge.

Two flower-filled tubs guarded the doorway. In the half-light, I could just make out the tell-tale soil ring of a recently moved pot. I crouched down to lift the heavy terracotta. Voila!

I snatched the golden Yale key and inserted it into the lock. "Brain not brawn works every time!" I joked. Nursing their bruised shoulders, my friends failed to find it funny.

"Okay, where are you all hiding?" Lakeisha marched through the hall into the kitchen, hitting all the light switches on the way. Ruben ran through upstairs, slamming open doors and firing up the national grid. Soon we had illuminated and explored every corner of the small house, but there was no sign of the Scooby-Don'ts or any of the psychic society. There was no one there except the four of us.

Elizabeth settled in the chair Muriel had used earlier. Ruben examined it for trigger devices, trap doors and wires. The cowled nun edged away from him as he curled around her feet.

"I'm not going to touch you." Ruben huffed.

I reached out to reassure her. "Elizabeth, please just let him look at the seat. He wants to see how you did this."

"Did what?" She shivered. "Prithee may I rest here. Mother Abbess and the community shall be up for matins soon. They shall be overjoyed to seeth me safe, and shall thank thee for thy good care of my person."

"Ruben, forget the chair!" Lakeisha dragged him away. "Google 'matins'. You were the only one with a signal in this outpost earlier."

Ruben threw his trusty rucksack on the kitchen table and slid out his tablet from one of its many compartments. "That's because I use the best provider. I spent weeks researching, adding up the pros and cons. Nothing below 100Mbps for me."

"Too much nerd." Lekeisha often used playful insults to disguise her amorous feelings. "Just pull up the internet."

My friends stationed themselves at the far end of the table whilst I pulled up another chair to sit beside Elizabeth. "May I?" I rested my hand on the edge of her knee, open palm facing to the ceiling with a hope that she would take it. Her freezing fingers cupped and twisted mine until they locked together. "You feel cold. Do you want a warm drink? Tea? I can put the kettle on." In the old hearth stood an aga range, but there was no time to fuss trying to work that out. Earlier we'd used an electric kettle brought by one of the other groups. If we were going to have a cup of tea, then I would need to heat the cups in the microwave.

Elizabeth appeared transfixed by the whirring sound of the motor. It was as if the revolving plate was sending her into a trance. Her eyelids drooped and her head bobbed.

"Is she nodding off?" Lakeisha whispered.

Ping!

"Where am I?" A startled Elizabeth edged her chair forward. "Who art thou?"

"No, we're not going over all that again!" Ruben stormed across and took my place in the chair opposite the confused 'nun'. "We're in the cottage where your mates switched you over with the bat-shit crazy medium as some kind of prank. And at 'matins'..." He made two bunny ears signs with his fingers. "At two a.m. your friends will shout surprise! And we will all have a flaming good laugh about all this. But right now, you are seriously winding me up!"

Lakeisha puffed up her chest in appreciation of this male bravado. Not quite a knight in shining armour moment, but there were still definite points scored. I thought it best to ease the tension by bringing the subject back to a nice cup of tea. "Do you take yours with milk and sugar?" I asked.

"Sugar? Pardon me, Mistress, thou hast sugar?" The very concept of my offering the sweet stuff agitated her.

"Yes, for the tea?" This explanation failed to address her concern. I dangled a tea bag over the cup of microwaved water.

"Thou means to poison me with those black herbs!" Elizabeth sprang from her chair and ran to the hall. "Mother Abbess! Sister Agnes! Help me!"

I started after her, but Ruben pulled me back. "Let her go! She's being dramatic. Playacting, remember? I say we get out of here. Technically, we are trespassing."

"Didn't you see her face? I think she's really terrified."

"You mean she's really talented. Tabs, it's a bad joke that's gone way too far." Lakeisha threw her arm across the doorway, barring my exit. "Let her go. When she realises we aren't following, she and the rest of them will come back and fess up." She paused, one hand on her hip and the other drumming on the frame. "I hate to say it, but Ruben is right. We shouldn't be in here. Let's wait for them outside."

I agreed. "Hold on… Did you hear her leave?"

The three of us leaned forward and poked our heads into the hallway. A crumpled pile of blue velvet lay at the end by the front door. Lakeisha and I nudged Ruben forward.

"Why me?"

"Because you're brave and strong!" Lekeisha tiptoed her fingers along his chest.

Ruben shrugged her off. "Yeah, right, and if I touch her, she'll cry rape!"

"Now who's being dramatic!" Lekeisha furrowed her brow, folded her arms across her bosom, and tutted. Her gaze fixed hard on Ruben. In that moment, the sexual tension of earlier evaporated into frustrated disappointment.

"Will you two get a room!" I squeezed past them both and crept down the hall. I knelt down by the velvet form, but it was empty. "Just the cloak!" I gathered up the soft blue material and walked back towards the kitchen. "She's maybe hiding somewhere in the house."

"Well, we're not looking for her. Her friends can find her at two a.m. I'm sick of this nonsense. Come on. Ruben, go get your bag. I'm getting out of here."

"What shall we do with this?" I folded up the cloak. There was a strange odour, it reminded me of the family dog.

"Leave it on the kitchen table."

I put down the cloak and turned my attention to the cups in the microwave; tossed the warm remains of the tea into the sink, rinsed them out and grabbed a tea towel.

"Hurry, Tabs! This place gives me the creeps!"

"I'm drying up. Just give me a sec!" I put the final cup back in the cupboard. The cabinet door slammed shut, just missing my fingers.

Everything plunged into darkness.

The Hounds were back.

"TABS! Tabitha! Ruben, she's coming round. Call an ambulance!"

Supportive arms lifted me up to my feet. The world was spinning and the shadowy blobs around me refused to focus.

"Everything is fuzzy." I complained.

"Thou hast had a shock, rest awhile to get thy bearings."

My eyes strained to zero in on the hand squeezing my right arm. Everything was a blur, but those nails weren't my friend's manicured creations.

Shapes sharpened around me. There was the kitchen table with the cloak still folded. By the door I could make out Lakeisha's purple scarf. Then a few seconds later, her face formed crystal clear. Ruben stood in the opening, his rucksack thrown over one shoulder. The other shoulder was propping up a familiar form.

That's me!

No one is accustomed to seeing themselves from behind, but that was my jacket, those were my jeans. I must have hit my head. This had to be some form of disassociation. An emotional response to the stress of the evening. My friends needed to slap me or something, to snap me out of it.

"Keish!" I cried. "Ruben!"

"They cannot hear ye."

I followed the voice.

"Elizabeth?"

"Welcome, Mistress Tabitha."

Ha-de-ha-ha! The trick's on me. Lakeisha and Ruben must have been in on it. April fools! They had dressed someone else in my clothes. What an elaborate plan! The mad nun and I must be behind a screen. I raised my fists and tried to pound on the glass, but my hands fell through the air in front of me. There was no screen, no wall.

"Come, rest awhile. We have an eternity for ye to understand."

Elizabeth guided me away from the kitchen. The stove and cupboards melted into a warm pink haze. A few more steps and the mist took on the golden hue of creamy yellow stone. Lavender and jasmine floated on the night air. We were in a verdant garden lined on every side by tall gothic arches. A fountain stood at the centre of the quad, and each square held rows of green-leafed vegetables or flowery herbs. Small torches lit the walls of the cloisters. And the full moon overhead bathed everything it touched in a silver sheen.

"It shall soon be matins. Just follow my lead. Thou shalt find peace here."

"I do not understand. How? Why?"

"They brought ye here."

"Who brought me here? Didn't you do this?"

I must be dreaming. That's the only rational explanation. I wasn't here. I was tucked up in my bed. In my digs. Sleeping off the side effects of a dodgy kebab we'd grabbed on the way home. This entire night was just a meat-induced acid trip.

"The Hounds."

"The Hounds?"

"Yes." Elizabeth clapped, and four black lumps of dribbling fur appeared from the far corners of the garden. "They aren't as fierce as their reputation. Like all creatures, they crave affection."

"But they were chasing you?"

"Well, they be hellhounds, that's what they do; drag sinners to hell."

"You are a nun!"

"I was."

"I don't understand. Am I in hell?"

"Of course not!" The hellhounds curled themselves at Elizabeth's feet, each pleading to have her tickle their stomachs. She crouched down to oblige. "Come, they don't bite."

I sat down on a flagstone, and a fluffy black head nuzzled its way onto my lap. His silky ears were warm and soft and comforting. "So, where am I?"

"I cannot answer that. There are others here. Sometimes they liveth in my world, they go about the convent and attend to its care. Other days I visit them. Sister Agnes prefers to live in her quaint little cottage, and Mother Abbess hath her own wing in a beautiful Norman chateau. We shall call on them when thou art settled."

"Am I dead?"

"There is no death. Only eternal life."

"So this is heaven? But we have hellhounds…"

Elizabeth smirked. The fear that had stalked her face earlier had disappeared. "They like ye."

"Where is Muriel?" I asked.

"Was that her name? She hast returned. I think she shall enjoy her new life."

A bell rang. Elizabeth stood up and kicked a fold out of the hem of her habit. "We must go to prayer. Come, thou shalt meet the others."

Elizabeth covered her head with her cowl and proceeded with the dogs towards the sound of the bell.

If Muriel could go back, then so could I. "And what if I don't want to?"

Elizabeth stopped. "I'm afraid they have decided." She smiled at the dogs close at heel. "Thou art staying."

"But why me?"

"No one knows when it is their time, but the Hounds do." She paused and drew in a long silent breath.

"They had two choices tonight. The old woman was a mistake. She would not be good company. She hast taken your place. You hath taken hers."

Turning, she added, "Thou treated me kindly. This," Elizabeth opened her arms, "everything here, is my gift. You will find peace and happiness. With me. With us. Forever."

She took my hands. "Please, after matins I shall ready thy quarters. Ye must tell me what is thy perfect home. I can make thee mistress of the alehouse, if you wish? Ye shall see, all shall be well."

"This is crazy! I'll get up in a minute and all of this will disappear." I pinched my arm as hard as I could.

Wake up, Tabs, wake up!

Two nuns appeared from the cloister. One with a large cross on a chain I took to be Mother Abbess, the other Sister Agnes. Other young women, clothed in varying fashions from different historical periods, followed. They encircled me, chanting.

"Welcome to St. Mildred's."

The aching grief in my heart told me this was not a dream.

Muriel has my life and I have this paradise for all eternity.

My family will not mourn me. Would they even notice I had changed?

The dog would know right? Animals can sense these things.

A warm snout pushed against my hand.

Mistress of the alehouse, eh?

I patted the hound's head and followed on behind.

The End

BLACK DEVIL SPAWN

A Jessamy Ward Mystery
The Isle of Wesberrey Series
A Short Story

BLACK DEVIL SPAWN

"Who are you looking at?" My weary, old eyes rest upon a motley youngster nervously cross-stepping her white socks in front of me like a crab on the harbour front.

"Why you, of course, Stranger!" She hisses. "That's a mighty fine coat you have there. All black and fluffy, no hint of rust, a few grey hairs though. Felix says black cats are the devil's spawn. And what happened to your face? Did something push your nose in?" She sniffs around me.

"I assure you, madam. I am no son of the devil. And my nose is beautiful. We have yet to be formally introduced. My name is Peregrine Pusscat the Third. Unlike you, I suspect, I can trace my lineage back at least three generations of Peregrine Pusses." I check her reaction. No sign of offence. Always hard to tell. Some cats have an inverted snobbery about us pedigree types.

My stomach growls.

I stretch and twist. *How long have I been curled under this tree?* It is very unlike me to fall asleep outdoors. My mind is foggy. I can't remember how I got here. *This isn't the family estate. What were those grey stones?*

"Do you have a name?" I ask politely. If I am to find my way home, I will need to get some local assistance, even if this feline before me is of the feral variety. Now was not the time to be particular.

"They call me Paloma, on account as I am mostly white, like a dove, my mother says."

"Charmed to meet you, Miss Paloma. May I ask you a question? It may seem rather silly, but I don't know where I am?"

"The church graveyard, back of St. Bridget's." Paloma tilts her head and gazes at me with a kitten-like wonder. "Where do you think you *should* be?" she asks.

"At home."

"And where's that?"

I look at Paloma, standing tall with that confident air of the young. I know I should know the answer. Lately, my mind has been so cloudy. Thoughts drift in and out and nothing feels solid. I want to say the cottage. But which one? *There are flowers. Pink and yellow flowers and thorns.* I think. *Roses! They're roses.*

"Rose Cottage?"

"Hmm, I don't know where that is, but Felix might. I'll take you to him." Paloma turns and curls her tail upwards. I fall in behind, my trailing tail bringing up the rear. *I hope it isn't far*. I feel faint.

The mossy earth smells of recent rain showers, not too damp, just enough to soften my steps. We wind our way through broken marble and small metal vials with dried out flowers. Green and yellow eyes look at us from the dusky recesses of the stones. *This is not my home. I do not belong here.*

The further inside we stroll, the more eyes fall upon us. From trees and tombs, shapes appear. There is a gathering of fur and claws. I don't want to look behind me. I know we are being followed. *Mummy will be so worried. My dinner will go dry, I hate when it does that.* I need to get my bearings again. Hopefully, this 'Felix' character will be a wise elder who can set me on my way.

The ways of the feral cats are a mystery to me. My mother always warned me to stay close by the cottage. *I love my mother.*

Mother says how lucky I am to be with her. She often speaks of other kittens. Beautiful greys and creams. Brothers and sisters the mistress took away.

"There are five of us at the cottage. My oldest sister, Trixibella Snowball is a champion white and my younger sister, Bella Luna, a beautiful blue."

"Just five of you?" Paloma seems impressed. "You must get so much to eat!"

"Yes, my bowl is always full." So w*hy do I feel so hungry?*

My mistress sits us by the fire grate, combing our hair each night. There is extra pampering before a show. As a boy, they spare me the ignominy of bows and diamante collars. How my sisters protest! Sometimes my mistress tugs too roughly, but never a cross word. *My coat feels so tight now, this will take hours to untangle!* Many other cats at the shows have terrible tales of their owners chastising them if they fail to win a rosette. *Maybe we are lucky?* There is always a coloured ribbon on my cage at the end of a show. At home, my mistress puts them on a corkboard and makes sure that all her visitors 'ooh' and 'aah' over the latest additions.

The show! I have to get back home. I have to prepare for the show.

Paloma stops in front of a large stone house, with magnificent columns and carvings of humans dancing on the walls. These humans are almost naked. *How weird they looked without fur.* The morning sun stretches its rays along the icy walls, lighting up the images in its path with an orange glow.

"Stay here. Felix will be here soon. The Wesberrey Clowder will take care of you." Paloma giggles and backs away.

Thank goodness, I don't think I could take another step. I look behind me. There is a glaring of cats. Despite Paloma's assurances, the Wesberrey Clowder do not appear to be the caring type. I don't want Paloma to go.

"Wait! Where are you going?" The meow sticks in my throat like an obstinate hairball. "Please, don't leave me!"

Paloma turns and dips her angled head. "What are you afraid of, Grandad?" She softly steps towards me and nuzzles her forehead against my shoulder. She purrs. "They won't harm you. I promise. Relax. We're like cousins, right? I have to go to the harbour now, the fishing boats are in and it's my turn, you see. I can't miss my slot or all I will eat is that awful tinned food from the parish. Unless it's tuna, we all love it when it's tuna."

"Fish from the boats?" My stomach rumbles. *When did I last eat?* "You eat fresh from the boats?"

"We take turns, there ain't enough for us all these days. Legend has it that long ago the dock teemed with each morning's catch. A time when the fishermen didn't chase us away because there was plenty. Now we rely on the parish."

Stop talking about food! My mouth is dry. My head feels woozy. I can hear Paloma is still talking but I cannot focus.

"When I was small, a kindly man dressed in black with a white collar around his neck, like a dog's. Actually, a lot like yours, He opened the tins. He ain't been here for a while, though. Lately, it's a single woman with short yellow hair and things dangling from her ears you just want to paw, you know? Don't know why she wears them if she doesn't want us to touch them. I mean, what else are they for?"

"My mistress has those things in her ears too." Why does thinking about my mistress make me feel sad? I try to remember, but it feels so long since I've seen her. *Fresh fish?* My mind whirls, trying to recall when I last ate fresh anything. "My mistress gives us these delicious small egg-shaped balls of food. The cat on the bag they come in looks just like my mother. My mother is so beautiful." *It feels so long since I've seen my mother.*

"Did she have a flat face like yours? It's a look, I suppose. Listen, Perry, I can't stay. Okay? There won't be nothing left. Felix will be here soon. He'll help you, for a price. Just none of that poncey talk ok? About bows and stuff."

I nod. *For a price?* My eyes follow her tail as she leaps up and across the stones that edge the yard until her last jump into the sun that is rising above the church wall.

The rest of the Wesberrey Clowder snake around me, looking me up and down like the judges at the shows. Paloma is right, surely these multicoloured moggies mean no harm. They are curious, that's all. They have probably never seen a cat of my breeding before. What would my mother tell me to do? *"Stand tall, Peregrine, stand tall. Nose up. Tail high."* I close my eyes. Let them look. *"Pedigree, Peregrine. Like your father and his father before him. Prize winners. Best in show. Stand proud, my son."*

I feel a sadness. It is evasive, like that feathery thing on the cane my mistress taunts me with. I can't pin it down. Something is wrong. Something is terribly wrong. I try to catch my thoughts and sit with my feelings for a moment. Just when I have them in my sight, they spring away. They tease me, darting this way and that. Never staying still. I am tired of the chase. I don't want to stand anymore. I want to roll up in a ball. I'm so hungry I can't think. *If Paloma is wrong, if these feline felons want to eat me, so be it.*

I flop. I curl. I cover my eyes.

A ginger paw nudges my nose.

"A Persian, eh? Slumming it a bit, aren't we, old man?" I raise my head to see a large tomcat with one emerald green eye looking down at me, his other eye lost in some distant catfight. From the scar, I imagine this was a hoary war wound.

Ah yes, I am lost in a graveyard. This must be the legendary Wesberrey Clowder Chief. I need his help. Straighten up, son.

"Are you Felix?"

"I sure am. And who's asking?"

"My name is Peregrine Pusscat the Third." I lumber up on all fours.

Felix moves closer, his shoulders broad, his eye focused. I shrink back. "No need to stir yourself, old-timer. That's quite the moniker you have there, eh? The gang here tells me young Paloma found you. I don't suppose she offered you anything to eat?"

I shake my head. *I met Paloma earlier this morning. I think. I think it was this morning? Paloma, white with splashes of orange.* These poor wild things have so little; I don't want to impose upon their hospitality, but my stomach speaks for me. Felix looks at two male tortoiseshells to his right, both shaped like they have enjoyed many a tinned tuna. Between them, they drag out a large brown oak leaf from a crevice in the base of the stone mausoleum, covered in jellied meat chunks. They put the leaf in front of me. I sniff. It smells like chicken.

"Go on, eat! You look like you need a good meal. Then we talk, okay?"

Felix sits back on his hind legs, his front paws in full regimental order.

"Will you help me? Paloma says you will know where I live. I have to get back, you see. It's very important." *Why is it important? It is, of course. Mother must be so worried. My mistress, too.* Felix stays silent. The other tomcats, watching from the shadows of fallen tree branches and crumbling headstones, crouch low, their tails flicking in jagged syncopation, prepared to pounce.

The chunks are larger than my usual kibble balls. I nibble away at the smallest one. *Oh my! It feels so good!* I am full after only a few mouthfuls. *What's the etiquette here? Will they be offended?* I gulp down as much as I can, hoping it's not customary to belch my gratitude or some other uncouth display of thanks.

"Thank you, but I can't eat any more, I'm sorry."

"Often the way with strays. When was the last time you ate, old timer? Do you remember?" I want to answer, but again the mew locks itself in my throat. I don't know. I don't know when I last ate. *The show!* "Shall we try to take you back

STEVEN HIGGS & PENELOPE CRESS

home? Can you remember where that was?" Felix's eye squinted in the afternoon sun.

It must be winter; the ancient star sits low in the sky. I feel restless. Not fearful, just distressed.

"There are roses. Pink and yellow. A gravel path. Lavender. There's lavender along the side of the path."

"Hmm, well that narrows it down to about a hundred different gardens on the island! Anything else? A pond, perhaps? One of those ugly fishing men things. They give me the creeps!" Felix shivers. I rack my brain. *I must remember something, it's my home, I have never lived anywhere else.*

"Catnip!"

"Ooh, now you're talking. Your garden has catnip?" Felix raises his paw to his mouth and licks it with his pink tongue. "Continue. Very few gardens grow their own, you know. Does your home have a dog? A fence? A sprinkler?"

"No, I don't think so. I don't recall a dog. Surely, I would remember a dog!" My thoughts are dancing around again. "Flowers. Purple, lilacs, yellow, white and green. And pink, a lot of pink."

"Let's go back to the catnip. Where do they grow that? Try to picture it in your mind. Is it in a container or a border?"

I know Felix is trying to help, but the pictures swim in and out.

"I'm sorry. I can't. I..."

Before I can finish, I see Felix's arm coming at me. He swipes at my nose. Claws out.

I flinch. He catches the corner of my ear.

"Meow!"

"Sorry, old man." Felix licks my blood off his paw. "It's a

nasty habit of mine. The boys always say I need to be more patient." He looks around at the circle of mangy mouse catchers, their eyes fixed upon me. They nod in creepy unison. "You were saying… the catnip."

I stutter. "The c-c-catnip… yes, there is. I'm sure there was… Tall stems, taller than me. Purple. brown-green leaves, coarse like tiny triangles" *There were other plants, herbs, mint and rosemary, in a large wooden box.* "My mistress used to shoo me away." My heart crumples. *My mistress, where are you? Why am I here? How did I get here?* "And there is a well! By a stone wall."

Felix lifts his hind legs and struts up and down before me.

"Sounds like Mildred Carmichael's cottage on the corner of Love Lane. You didn't stray far, did you?" The ginger tom stares me down with his one good eye. "Well, if you're fed, I say we all take a little stroll up to the Carmichael's. See if we can't get ourselves a little of that good stuff. As a reward, you understand, for bringing her beloved Periwinkle the Fourth home from his wanderings."

"Peregrine. My name is Peregrine *the Third*."

"Whatever." Felix leads the way, and I follow meekly behind, guarded on all sides by the rest of his gang. The sun is setting now, and it will soon be dark. *What would my mistress think of an army of alley cats invading our little home?* Another wave of sadness washes over me. I swallow down a lump in my throat. The feeling that something has happened echoes in my mind, but what it is remains just beyond my grasp.

At the cemetery gate, a cluster of queens and kittens are preening themselves on a moss-covered stone slab. I can see Paloma reclining against the corner, her left leg pointing up toward the sky, her tongue seductively flicking the fur of her inner thigh. Felix stops to admire the scene.

"Well, well, ladies. Need any help with your beauty regime?" he chuckles.

"Move along now, Felix!" An elderly she-cat, with a broken tail and a large patch of black fur covering both eyes like a masked supervillain, moves in between us and the bathing beauties. "Plenty of time for that after dark. My ladies need a rest, you know."

"Fair enough, Queenie. We have business with Prince Puss-in-boots here. A garden with its own catnip. The boys will be frisky when we return." Felix saunters over to Paloma. She rubs her head against the stone, rolling her slender frame around with an exaggerated wiggle of her hind legs. She stops, tail erect, and pushes her chest down to the ground, stretching her front paws out and raising her rear towards the approaching leader of the pack. Felix quickens his pace. Queenie skips in front and blocks his way.

"Tonight, tiger! You know she will be worth the wait."

Queenie hisses at Paloma, who slinks away behind the stone.

As I walk out of the graveyard, there are familiar chimes floating on the air. Bells, the church bells. I must live close by. *Maybe my mistress is Mildred Carmichael?* I know her as 'Mummy'. *Mummy will be so happy to see me safely home.* What is a little catnip to repay their kindness?

We amble along the country lane that runs alongside the flint wall of the cemetery. It must be winter. The trees are bare. The darkening sky is grey. The wind twists at my fur. *Mummy will be so angry if my coat is all matted.* My mother will tell me off too. She always tells me and my sisters how important it is to always look our best. *Why do these thoughts hurt?* There's a dull pain in my chest. An emptiness almost as bad as the hollow feeling in my stomach. It grows with every weary step I take.

"Tell me, Prince Pawfect, about your fancy-pants house-hold. What is life like at the Carmichael's? Do you drink from silver bowls? Does the butler serve your dinner? And the ladies…" Felix stops sharply and turns, "Those pedigree ladies, you must have been put out to sire, a handsome chap like you."

"Would you believe me if I say I can't remember?"

The Clowder Chief stares me down with his one eye. "No" he snaps, then softens. "I would say you are being the gentleman they raised you to be. I admire that." The other cats in our unlikely party mock me with calls of 'fancy-pants' and 'la-de-dah'. Felix doesn't stop them. I want to be back home, by the fire. *Mummy will stroke my chin. I like that.*

"As chief, I always get first pickings." Felix flexes his tail. "That Paloma, such a fine kitten, isn't she? She is so ready. I'll be biting down hard on her pretty little neck tonight, high on the good stuff and savouring every moment." Felix curls his tail in anticipation. "The rest of you boys can have her afterwards!"

My bodyguard cheers raucously.

I think about all the female cats in my life. My mother and my sisters. I shudder to think of them at the paws of these ruffians. *Just lead them to the catnip and move them on as quickly as possible.*

"Well, here we are, this is the Carmichael's cottage. There is the well. The roses. Does it look familiar?"

I step carefully out of the group and stand in front of the wooden gate. I'm not sure. I usually stay close to the house. I am rarely outside the garden fence. Only when we go to a show, or to the vet's or the groomer's and then I am in my crate. I don't want to let on that I'm not sure. My ear is still smarting from last time. *Perhaps if I go through the gate?*

I slink under the bottom bar. On the other side is a gravel path. There are twigs of old lavender bushes growing at the side, but the path itself is not as clear as I remember. Dried husks of dandelions pepper the ground before me. The thorns of the rose bushes are stretching out at all angles and the lawn grass is high and untamed.

The mewing of my companions rises in volume until I can hardly hear myself think. Within seconds, the Wesberrey Clowder cats are exploring every inch of the garden. Their frustration growing louder and louder. I feel a heavy paw on my tail.

"So, where is it? Where is the catnip?" Felix rounds and takes a second swing at me with his open paw. This time I am more prepared and pull my face back into my neck, arching my back and scuttling my feet back to withdraw to a safe distance. *Stand proud, my son.*

"Felix, I'm not sure this is the right house. It looks different. The plants are wilder. The paint on the gate, the door? Yet, it looks familiar..." Felix is unamused by my ramblings. He primes his claws, ready for another strike. His hissing minions circle around me. *They want the good stuff.* "Maybe the catnip is in the back garden?" I suggest.

"You had better hope for your sake that it is. The boys are getting impatient. They don't like cats who welch on their promises." Felix points to the back of the house with his muzzle and members of the gang scamper up the side fence and work their way towards the rear of the cottage.

"There's a cat flap in the side door. Follow me."

I'm not sure why I said that. I think there is a door with a hinged plastic flap. Part of me wants to be wrong. *This cannot be my house.* This place is little better than a derelict shed set in a bramble wood. But there is the door and the flap.

"Well," growls Felix, "You go first!"

No, it can't be my house. I hope they are out - my sisters, my mother. Don't worry. Mummy will take a broom to these rapscallions.

I push through the dusty plastic cover. It opens, as it has always opened, into the kitchen. *This is my house.* My paws set down upon the familiar black-and-white chequered lino floor. Ahead through an open door is the front parlour. The fireplace where Mummy brushes my fur is cold. White sheets cover the furniture. The curtains are drawn, and a thin layer of dust coats every surface.

"So, is there another cat flap in the back?"

I turn slowly to Felix and nod.

This is my house, but Mummy isn't here anymore. My mother and father, my sisters... No one is here anymore. I have pushed open the cat flap in my mind and memories crowd in. *I remember.* I am alone. I remember Mummy on the floor of the kitchen. I kept nuzzling at her hand. I was hungry. She hadn't moved for days. She was cold. It had been just me and her for a while. She wasn't able to comb my matted coat anymore. Her hands couldn't hold the brush.

There is no show. There have been no shows for a long time. No trips to the vet or the groomer. My mistress never went out anymore. I stayed with her as much as I could. I remember. *I remember.*

Squeals from the back of the house tell me that Felix and the gang have found the catnip. I take my chance and sneak back out through the flap in the side door and quietly make my way back towards the graveyard. *Maybe they will let me stay, as I brought them to catnip heaven? Maybe they will let me live quietly on the outskirts of the cemetery? I don't need a lot to eat, I will take the scraps.* I pass the she-cats and tell them the boys would be back soon.

The night is drawing in. Paloma takes me to a vacant spot outside the cemetery where I can sleep for the night. I resolve to talk to Felix in the morning. Beg him to let me stay. *Where else can I go? Who wants an ancient tomcat with no mousing skills and a matted fur coat?*

"I have lost everything," I tell her. Paloma nuzzles me gently and promises she will put in a good word for me that night. I am sure she will be very persuasive. I fear for her, but she is young, resilient. She has something Felix wants, for now. *I am an old fool to think I can stay.* They have the catnip. The house is empty. No one to shoo them away. I have nothing left to bargain with.

I curl up under an old tree stump. The night air wraps its icy embrace around me. The ground is cold. Carolling tomcats, high on the good stuff, return to a noisy night of feline pleasure. I hope that the dark night will cloak me until morning. I shiver. My heart lies shattered in my chest, pierced through with a thousand crystal needles. *I remember. I am alone. I* try to muffle my whimpers of grief. They cannot find me. It will be a long, lonely night.

DAWN BREAKS. After a night of revelry, the Wesberrey Clowder are slow to rise. I take advantage of their slumber to stretch my legs. My thoughts run to the fisherman's catch. I would like to eat fresh fish before I die. *Just a taste. That would be nice. Maybe I could hide out there on the docks.*

My musings are interrupted by the distinct sound of footsteps crossing the graveyard.

The other cats stir. I can see Paloma on the far side of the graveyard. Her silky smooth white coat grey and sticky from the passions of the night before.

I don't belong here.

A woman dressed in black, her hair caught up in a sort of human tail, wearing what looks like a collar like mine, stumbles through the headstones. She stops outside the big mausoleum. The one with the humans dancing. She shakes her head and tuts.

I lose sight of Paloma.

Felix and the others wrap themselves around the human's legs. At first, she seems startled and then becomes extremely apologetic. She runs off, sneezing. I want to escape with her. The Clowder follow. *I can't be seen.* There's a hole in the wall. I flatten myself into the crack and pray they pass me.

The human stops. She promises to be back soon with food. *Food!*

I am starving. All these thoughts of fish have made my

stomach ache for some nourishment, but I cannot go out. I must stay hidden.

The tomcats are angsty, scratching around for a fight. *Please move on! I'm too old, too tired. Leave me here. I will die in this hole. There is nothing to live for anyway.*

"Psst!"

A gentle paw strokes my back. I didn't think anyone could see me from the lane side of the wall. *I am a stupid old fool!*

"Go with her!"

I squirm around to face the other way. It's Paloma.

"Please, leave me alone." I see a pain in her almond eyes that wasn't there the night before. The kitten is now a queen.

"They will kill you if you stay. I tried. I really did, but…"

"You don't need to explain." I step out of my hiding space.

"The human with the tail has a kind face." *She does.* The other cats seem content to wait. Maybe this is my chance? Paloma licks my cheek tenderly. "Go, go now. I will distract them."

"Come with me?"

Paloma shakes her pretty head.

"I will visit, Grandad. Okay? When I do, let me in." She rounds and leaps up on the wall and saunters along the ridge. "Hey boys! What's a girl got to do to get some attention?" She jumps down to a choir of excited squeals.

I crawl out past the oak tree and slither down the lane, weaving through the shadows, in pursuit of my prize.

I can hear my mother's voice lifting me up as I run. *"Stand proud, my son"*.

I am no alley cat!

I'm not designed to slink about hoping for titbits and leftovers!

I am a champion.

I have a corkboard full of blue rosettes.

I am running after that human and I am having a proper meal, in a proper bowl in a proper kitchen. Humans love me. I will make her love me.

She is fiddling with some metal trays and tins of cat food at the back door of the vicarage when I catch up to her. I follow her into the kitchen.

This is a lovely kitchen. There are flowers on the table. I sniff the air. There are other humans here. I sniff again. No dogs. *Perfect!* The aga reminds me of my old home. It is warm. Inviting. And the floor is of black-and-white chequered tiles.

Stand proud, my son.

I jump up onto a wooden chair and from there onto the table. I sit up as straight as possible. This is not an occasion for slouching. This is the show of shows and I am best of breed!

"Okay, okay, I will feed you first." The woman in black awkwardly scoops out the fishy contents of a small tin onto a green saucer. I make short work of it and snuffle it down. *Lovely small chunks, perfect for my delicate mouth.*

"Do you want some more? I guess you are really hungry."

Almost there. This will be my new home. Just a cute lick of the lips and…

She pats me on the head.

She wants me to get off the table. Coaxes me. Tries to grab me, but I wriggled free.

She laughs. She wants to get me to go back with her to feed my 'friends'.

I look around the cosy kitchen. I'm not going anywhere.

"Fine. Stay here." She sneezes. *How sweet!* "Check the

place for mice, whilst I'm gone." *Oh, there're mice too! This will do nicely, very nicely indeed.*

She walks to the door.

Look back, look back.

She turns.

"I think I'll call you Hugo."

Hmm, Hugo? Better than Peregrine, I suppose. Take that, Felix! Not bad for black devil spawn, eh?

This is my house now.

The End

JUBILEE JINKS

A Prequel - Just Following Orders

A Jessamy Ward Mystery
The Isle of Wesberrey Series
A Short Story

1

JUBILEE JINKS

"So, tell me again how hard you fought against being posted back to that forsaken little island?"

"Mum, I promise you I protested as much as I could but once Bishop Marshall has an idea in his head there is no talking him out of it."

"But surely you have some say in where you live and work? And why there? I have a very bad feeling about going back there. Nothing good on Wesberrey except your aunts. Only bad memories and feral cats!" Mum piled up my plate with more cake as if fattening me up was her secret weapon against my returning to the place of my birth.

"Go on, Aunt Jess, Tell us again how you found out," Clara asked.

"Do I have to put on the voice?" I looked at my two nieces, both sitting like bookends on the far corners of Mum's sofa.

"Yes. Does he really talk like that?"

"Freya, my darling girl. I'm afraid he does." I took in a

deep breath and in a melodic voice continued. "Reverend Jessamy Ward!" Only Bishop Marshall, or my mother, ever called me Jessamy. "I think it's time for you to have your own parish. The vicar on the Isle of Wesberrey passed away a few months ago. Terrible end, pancreatic cancer, most unpleasant. Anyway, God has welcomed him home and his happy departure leaves a vacancy that, well, if I am honest, no one else is overly keen to take on." The Bishop had the most unusual, sonorous voice that made everything he said sound like a Gregorian chant. "I understand you know that godless outpost, still have family there and such like. It will be a challenge. Mainly ageing hippies, crusty old fishermen and eccentric misfits, but I am sure you will do your best."

"I am not sure Aunt Cynthia would like to be referred to as an ageing hippy!" My mum grumbled. "And Pamela even less. I doubt there is a more *conservative* hippy on the planet. Do hippies buy their clothes in Marks and Spencers?"

"Maybe she's a crusty old fisherman!" Freya joked.

"Er hum, you asked me to do this. Please don't interrupt."

"Sorry, Reverend."

"Ok, where was I? Ah, yes. Then I said 'And cats, you forgot the colony of feral cats'" I returned to my sing-song impersonation. "Ah yes, the cats! Colin used to complain that they would keep him awake all night fighting in the graveyard."

"Forget the bloody cats! It's the human pests you have to worry about!" My mother had grown up on Wesberrey, as had generations of her family before her, but the sudden death of my father made her take me and my sisters away when I was a teenager. Now I was sat in her front room sharing the news of my new parish with her and two of my three nieces. The news of my return to the Island was getting a mixed reception.

"I did try, Mum. I told him, 'Your Grace, I'm not sure this is the right posting for me. I do have some family left there but I haven't seen much of them over the years. My mother took us away when I was a teenager, and I have no desire to return there.'"

"An island full of cats. It sounds perfect for sad lonely spinsters," I eyed Freya with a look that made it clear I was not happy with her little joke. "Not that you're a sad lonely spinster, Aunt Jess. You are just... fussy."

"Selective." Chimed in Clara, desperate as the older sister, to save her sibling from further embarrassment.

"Sensible. That's what your Aunt Jess is. Unlike your mother throwing herself at anything in trousers. Every time she swore it was forever. Where is she now? Deepest, darkest Peru saving Paddington's relatives, just because what's-his-name is the one. Again."

Clara now had to leap in to defend her absent mother. "Mum's in Brazil with Federico. She's as passionate about the plight of the buffy-headed marmosets as he is."

"Of course, dear. At least I don't have to worry about her turning up at my door pregnant anymore. That's something. More tea? I think we all need a top-up."

And with that Mum collected up the mugs and took herself out to the kitchen. My older sister Zuzu (or Susannah as my parents had named her) had struggled to settle down with one man. I was not convinced that was ever her intention. She wasn't one to be confined to one spot for long. Although, she had managed to stay put long enough to get pregnant on three separate occasions. The results were my beautiful nieces, Clara, Phoebe and Freya.

"Anyway," I continued, keen to change the subject, "I told him that I was hoping for an inner-city parish where I can bring God's love to troubled youths, isolated pensioners, the lost and the lonely. And as for the cats... I'm allergic!"

"Of course. I'd forgotten. Surely you could appeal on health grounds?"

"Dear Clara, always the one with the sensible head on her. That is a great idea but probably too late now." Morphing back into a medieval monk I continued. "This is a great opportunity, Jessamy. You can bring God's love to a community who have turned their backs on him. They are truly lost. God is calling you. You are the only man, I mean, woman for the job." You see, my beloved nieces, at that point I knew that I had no choice. I would be returning to Wesberrey. 'And what about the cat allergy?' I asked. Do you know what he answered? 'Take some antihistamines!' "

Freya smiled at the Bishop's helpful suggestion. "So, when do you have to move in then?"

"Won't be for a few months yet. I think I will be able to spend Christmas at home here and then they should set my collation and induction for the end of January. These things take time. I have to be approved by the parish council first."

"Oh, they will love you just as much as we do." Freya jumped out off the sofa and perched herself on the arm of my chair before giving me a hug. Because of my sister's many adventures in pursuit of love it had fallen to my mother to be the main caregiver to her three granddaughters. When they were younger, Zuzu used to take them with her - always moving on to a new home, a new life. My sister was a very loving mother but she always needed something more. When Clara started secondary school, my mother offered to take the girls in during term time. Just to give them a little stability. Let them settle down. Make friends. Zuzu would visit between adventures and the girls went to her in the school holidays. It was an arrangement that seemed to suit everyone - especially my mother. Now the youngest, Freya was at university. The house was quiet again.

"Aunt Jess, how much do you remember of the Island? Apart from the cats, that is. We've only met Grandma's sisters a few times. I don't think Freya remembers the last time they were here."

"All I know is that Mum says that Cynthia is away with the fairies. Thinks she's a witch, has a gingerbread house and everything! I'll go help Grandma."

Freya stepped out to the kitchen and returned with my mother and even more cake. As they settled back down I racked my brain to remember the strange island I was soon to call my home for a second time.

"Well Clara, I remember it was a pain to get anywhere because there are no cars. Your mother's first boyfriend...what was his name, Mum?"

"How am I supposed to remember that, there's been so many!"

"Trevor! That was it."

"Trevor!" both of my nieces laughed. Trevor was not the most exotic of names. Zuzu's current beau was Frederico but there had been a Johannes, Xavier and a Vladamir.

"Yes, Trevor. Nothing funny about that. He had a new

53

Honda scooter. That made him quite the catch. And long hair. I remember he had *very* long hair. Well, it was the seventies."

"How old was she? Clara, remember she made us swear not to date till we were sixteen."

"Er, she might have been a tad younger. I know she was with him during the Jubilee. What year was that?"

"1977. Zuzu was fourteen. Your grandfather was not impressed. He banished your mother to her bedroom and threatened to keep her there until she turned eighteen."

"She got out anyway." I giggled with the memory of my older sister sneaking out across the conservatory roof. "Yes, '77. That was the year I went to big school off the island in Oysterhaven. I would have been eleven and Rosie, bless her, was about eight."

Rosie was our youngest sister. She was easily the most sensible of the three of us and had been married now to Teddy for twenty years. They had one son, Luke. There was a strange pattern in my family. One sister would have three daughters, one would have a son and the other, well, the other, like me and my aunt Cynthia were born to not have any children of our own. According to family folklore that was because the childless sister was destined to be the appointed keeper of the Well of the Triple Goddess on Wesberrey. Total nonsense, of course. I was sure it was just a coincidence but it was pretty weird.

"The Jubilee?" Freya looked confused, her freckles knotting together into small brown blobs.

"Yes, like back in 2002. The Queen had been on the throne fifty years then, well she had another jubilee twenty-five years earlier. You must remember her Golden Jubilee. Brian May on the roof of Buckingham Palace?"

Freya looked even more bewildered. "2002? I was a baby!"

I turned to Clara.

"Don't look at me, I was only seven. Who is Brian May?"

"Who is Brian? Queen? Freddie Mercury? C'mon. Bohemian Rhapsody?" At last, they nodded in recognition. "Okay, well what about the Diamond Jubilee then, that was only eight years ago?" They finally realised what I was talking about and I realised I was getting old. "Well, young whipper-snappers," I said in a mock 'old lady voice' "Make yourselves comfortable because I remember the summer of 1977 very well. It was the year Her Majesty, Queen Elizabeth II visited Wesberrey and things almost went terribly, terribly wrong."

2

CHARLIE'S ANGELS

"Once upon a time, there were three little girls who went to the Wesberrey School. And they were each assigned some very hazardous homework."

"It's not that bad. I quite like fractions."

"But that's because you're the smart one. Do you think we will be separated at St. Mildred's in September?"

My best friend Sam Simmons was brilliant at everything at school. She would have been the only one of the three of us to go to the girls' grammar school in Oysterhaven, St. Mildred's if they hadn't changed all the schools into comprehensives that year. The upside for me and our other best friend, Karen Clark was that now we could go to 'big' school with her. The Wesberrey Angels could stay together.

"I've heard that they stream you. They put you into classes according to how clever you are. So, Jess, you and I will be in the bottom set for everything!"

"Don't be daft you are great at English. You write such great stories."

We made a funny trio and really didn't look anything like the real Charlie's Angels, though we were huge fans of the tv show. Sam was tall, slim, bespectacled with a mischievous streak. She found school work unchallenging and often alleviated her boredom by finding ways to test the rules, never fully breaking them. Karen was medium build and height. I was easily the shortest as well as the youngest. I guess there was plenty of growing yet to do, we were still only eleven (well, technically I was ten, my birthday was a whole month away). I passionately hoped there was more growth to come because I admit I was a bit fed up with being the 'baby' of the group. Sam was the clever one, Karen the artistic and sporty one and I was, well, I wasn't particularly good at lessons, or sports or art, or music. That made me Kelly Garrett. Sam was Sabrina Duncan and Karen was Jill Monroe. Karen was the only blonde one in our gang so it had to be her. She was also the most athletic. If any of us was going to look good in a white tennis outfit scratching our behinds it was going to be Karen.

"Karen, look at your arms! You have a tan already. That's not fair. The sun's hardly been out so far this summer."

"Must have caught the sun when I was with the boys last weekend."

The 'boys' Karen was referring to were a gang of skateboarders who used the main road down from Upper Road to Market Square, Abbey Hill Drive, as their makeshift skate park. Karen hung out with them whenever she was fed up of playing with us. Neither Sam nor I were very interested in sports or *real* boys for that matter. Not yet anyway. I preferred my boys to smile at me from the posters on my wall.

"Your sister was there, Jess with her boyfriend. He brought his scooter. Yawn. The older boys took it in turns to ride it. They were all showing off. Don't see the point myself."

"The point of what? Showing off or riding the scooter?" Sam asked, genuinely curious. She often challenged us with such questions, as if we were part of some sociological research. "Surely getting around the Island quicker with minimal effort is clearly advantageous. As to showing off, that's what boys do, isn't it? Especially when there are girls around."

"Don't get me wrong, It wasn't all bad. Your sister had her new JVC radio cassette player with her so we had some music and that. Though some of it was a bit, well different." Karen pulled in closer and whispered so that my mother couldn't hear. "They were playing the Sex Pistols!"

It didn't work.

"Karen Clark! Wash your mouth out, young lady! What would your parents say? You don't use words like that in their house do you?" The serving hatch linking the dining room and the kitchen screeched open.

"No, Mrs Ward. I'm sorry. But that is the name of the group. Susannah and Trevor were playing it. I didn't like it very much. It was just shouting."

My mother extended her neck and head through the hatch.

"My Susannah? I knew that boy was trouble. Just wait till her father gets home. Anyway girls, it's very nearly tea time. You must be finished with that homework by now."

"Just a few more problems, Mum. Shouldn't take more than ten minutes. Promise."

"Well, then you might have some time for a little treat after supper. I have some Arctic Roll in the freezer. Would you girls like a slice each?" It was always my mother's way to bawl us out and then offer cake. This one had the added benefit of an ice cream centre.

After the desserts had been passed through the hatch, the spy hole was closed. Soon the comforting sound of my mother washing up as the tunes of 'The Manhattan Transfer' seeped through the small crack between the wooden doors. "*Chanson D'Amour... rat-ta-tat-te-tat..*"

"Karen?" I coughed "Do you think my sister is, you know, kissing Trevor?"

Karen laughed.

"I think they are doing a lot more than that!" Karen lowered her voice and leant in. "She sat on his lap when he was stationary on the scooter. He kept putting his hand down her blouse. She was hitting it away, of course, and giggling. There was a lot of giggling. All very boring if you ask me."

"Angels, do you think we will ever be like that? With boys that is, all giggly and stuff."

I looked at my friends. Sam sat back in her chair, pencil firmly locked between her teeth which meant she was giving the question serious consideration. Karen was more puzzled by the final sum in front of her. After a few minutes, Sam broke the silence.

"I can imagine that we will be no different from all those who have gone before us. There must be something to *it* if we,

STEVEN HIGGS & PENELOPE CRESS

as a species, keep on, you know, doing it. However, maybe science will come up with an alternative. I mean, this love business seems very messy. All those country and western songs make it sound so painful. Who would want to experience that?"

3

MORNING ASSEMBLY

Mr Forrest, our headmaster had gathered the whole school together for assembly. Each class lined up in alphabetical order by surname, in untidy columns facing the front and the stage. I waved at my sister Rosie from across the hall.

"Now, as you know children the Island is expecting a very special visitor here next Friday. Her most gracious Majesty, Queen Elizabeth will be passing by on the HMS Britannia and there will be a very brief stop at Stone Quay where she will disembark to receive our tribute for her Silver Jubilee." Mr Forrest was like both Father Christmas and the child catcher from Chitty Chitty Bang Bang at the same time. As one hand delved deep into his tweed jacket to hand you a cellophane covered mint as a reward, the other prepared itself to give you a swift clip round the ear in punishment. His mood today suggested there would be free mints for all. "I will hand you over to Mr Leybourne who will tell you what we need to do to prepare."

In all ways that mattered Mr Leybourne, the deputy head, was just a taller less hunched version of Mr Forrest. He too used rewards and punishments to control us but appeared to use more personal energy to enforce them. His face was always on the verge of turning as violently red as his temper.

As Mr Leybourne stood up to speak a surprised giggle caught fire across the hall. One disadvantage of having a surname beginning with the letter 'W' is that messages and gossip took a long time to reach you. There had been many times when I had embarrassingly laughed at a joke after the room had returned to silence.

"Sssshhh! Pass it on. Adrian Little saw Mr Leybourne and Miss Sykes snogging in the staff room this morning."

"Silence!" Mr Leybourne yelled.

I swallowed my surprised gasp.

"Adrian Little! I will see you in my office after assembly. Now, to her Majesty's visit."

It took Mr Leybourne far too long to explain the details of Her Majesty's trip. Most of his seemingly endless speech centred on how important it was to be on our best behaviour as we were representing not only ourselves but also him, Mr Forrest, our parents, the school and the whole of Wesberrey. The whole ceremony sounded quite boring. Lots of people standing around and a communal singing of 'God Save the Queen'. At least it meant a day out of lessons. The most interesting part was going to be the presentation to Her Majesty of a special commission created by the island's resident celebrity artist, Clifford Reid. Clifford Reid was an extraordinary character and the type of British eccentric most children would taunt and run away from. That was not an option for me as he was my aunt Cynthia's boyfriend.

I had visited his studio once. A fascinating place, full of misshapen lumps of clay that vaguely resembled people, if those people were like those plastic troll dolls with coloured hair. These objects were not dolls, though they looked like famous people from the television. Clifford had told me that one of them was the Prime Minister and the other was the American President, Jimmy Carter. My aunt said that they were all political statements against the establishment. Whatever that meant. To me, they looked funny, so I laughed. I remember my aunt and Clifford shaking their heads and saying something about she will understand one day. I wondered what his piece for the Queen would look like.

I awoke from my daydream to find Mr Leybourne was still talking. I think most of my fellow pupils were actually asleep.

"As Her Majesty's visit will be very brief, there will not be much time for us to see Mr Reid's work so Reverend Weeks has offered to display it over at the church and we will also go over after our assembly on Monday to take a look. The artist will be there to talk about what inspired him and answer any questions you may have."

After what seemed like forever we were finally released in our lines to return to class. Miss Sykes was our class teacher. She blushed as my sniggering classmates filed past to get to our desks. I liked Miss Sykes. She was young, pretty, always wore Laura Ashley style dresses and had fresh flowers on her desk. Like almost everyone else on Wesberrey, Miss Sykes cycled around the Island. I was very envious of her pastel green bicycle with its wicker basket at the front. I completely under-stood why Mr Leybourne would want to kiss her.

"Now class, please get your trays. The first lesson today is maths."

Each pupil had a coloured tray with their name on a sticker at the front. The trays contained all our educational tools: pencil cases filled with coloured pens, felt tips, Bic biros for those who had graduated up to them, and different coloured exercise books for every subject. Maths was orange and inside were pages filled with tiny squares. Maths work was always done in pencil which was just as well because I always had to rub it out and start again.

At my work table sat Sam and Karen, of course, but we were also joined by three of the 'boys'. Jonathan Brooker, whose rodent features already had acne, poor thing. Scruffy William Brown who was the only kid in class wearing brown leather shoes. The uniform was white shirts, red ties, grey trousers or pinafores and black shoes. William said the shoes were a present from his father. His father was away somewhere so Miss Sykes let him keep them on. The final boy at our table was Adrian Little, who was probably feeling the cold rubber sole of Mr Leybourne's 'slipper' on his backside as we sat down to open our books.

"Sam, Jess why don't you ever join us after school like Karen does. We have so much fun. Your sister brought her boyfriend the other day. He is so cool. Just like the Fonz. Aaaay!"

"Jonathan Brooker, get on with your work."

"Sorry, Miss!"

Adrian Little sheepishly entered Miss Sykes classroom,

apologised to her for being late, collected his tray and slunk into his chair. He didn't say a word for the rest of the morning but his teary eyes spoke for him. Later, at break time, the boys were gathered by the bike shed.

"I think we should go over and see if Adrian's ok?" Sam suggested.

"But I thought we were going to do some French skipping!" Karen grumbled. This game with elastics was the latest craze in the playground. Karen and Sam loved it. I think being the shortest had me at a disadvantage and I wasn't so keen.

"I'll go with you, Sam." I scuttled up behind my gangly friend and looked back at the other with my best 'come on, join us' face. "He did look really upset. D'you think Mr Leybourne was very angry?"

"Okay, you win. I'll come with you. You need three to skip anyway, so I have no choice really, do I?" With that Karen raced ahead. I think she was just pretending to not want to go over. Karen hated to be left out.

4

SKATER BOYS

"We're so going to get him back." Adrian's eyes were now red with anger rather than tears.

"Get who back?" I asked.

"Leybourne, of course. It's not right."

"So you did get the slipper then." It wasn't an actual slipper. That would be almost civilised. Mr Leybourne used a black gym plimsoll. For really bad offences he had been known to use his 'trusty' cane.

"So?" William asked, "What are we going to do?"

"Well, I have been thinking. We need to hit him where it hurts. Cause him so much embarrassment that he'll be forced to quit. Leave the school and the island and never return!"

"How, exactly, do you plan to do that Adrian Little, eh? Do you have any bright ideas in that gossipy head of yours?" Sam was a little too interested in where this conversation was going for my liking.

"I have as it happens, Miss Brainy Box. We are going to mess up the Queen's visit."

"And how, Mr Red Backside, do you suggest we do that?"

Sam and Adrian were now standing toe to toe. Eyes fixed. Hands on hips.

Miss Sykes blew her whistle.

Break time was over.

Well-drilled boys, who seconds before were running around in hot pursuit of their quarry with hands for guns, or playing football, joined equally obedient girls who slowly crossed the concrete playground to line up in rows to go back inside. Girls, who seconds before had been looking at music magazines, or singing rhymes and throwing balls against the school walls.

The school yard fell silent. Miss Sykes nodded and we walked back to our room.

Back in class, Adrian was given the task of handing out the round edge scissors. We were going to make red, white and blue paper chains.

"Meet me in the churchyard tonight at five o'clock. I have a plan."

"I DON'T THINK they are coming. They must have chickened out. All talk and no action. That's boys for you."

Karen kicked her shoes against one of the headstones. Nothing happens on Wesberrey and I think we were all looking forward to a little bit of adventure, still that didn't mean we had to misbehave.

"Stop that! Have you no respect. What if Reverend Weeks catches you or worse his boss!"

"What Him, you know God?" Karen suddenly stood very still and slowly moved her head to look over her right shoulder.

"No, you silly sausage, Reverend Cheeseman," I whispered "I hear that he once locked a boy in the bell tower for three days because he caught him folding down a corner of one of the prayer books to hold his place."

"What utter rubbish!" Sam lifted herself up onto one of the raised stone tombs and crossed her legs. "Though that boy thoroughly deserved to be punished for abusing a book like that."

The graveyard was a really creepy place to be. Very few funerals took place there anymore because my mother said it was full-up of bodies and if they dug any more holes for new ones, the old ones would rise up. Many of the headstones had collapsed into the ground. As there were few new inhabitants there were also hardly any mourners to maintain the graves. The most frequent visitors were the island's famous feral cats.

Every child is taught that the cats were brought in to protect the island's precious grain store in times of famine. With the local fisherman's bountiful catches and passing trade from merchant ships, this meant that the local community were historically able to weather any mainland food shortages. The cats were well cared for and prospered along with the island. When the plague hit the mainland, Wesberrey escaped death. That may have been because there were no rats or because we are an island cut off from the outside world but every child on the island knows that to harm a cat is to hurt your own family. Their population increased over the centuries and now outnumber the human population. Many of them live in and around the churchyard. In the morning they saunter down to the harbour to eat the spoils of the morning's catch and then they return to the tombs to bask in the midday sun. Visitors and tourists leave donations of cat food at the church but they don't really need it. They are well-fed moggies. They would be a very cute distraction as we wait but I can't go near them as they make me sneeze and my eyes stream like Niagara Falls.

Karen picked up a slinky black version and started to walk towards me.

"They say these fellas are unlucky. But this little one is so beautiful. Aren't you puss, eh? You are bootiful." Karen nuzzled her forehead against the cat. It was love at first sight.

"Just keep your new friend away from me. You know I'm allergic. Do you think the boys will come?"

Sam leant back on her cold platform and looked up at the sky.

"I knew that Adrian Little was all mouth and no trousers. Such a shame. I was beginning to have a bit of respect for him."

"More like you were beginning to have the hots for him." Karen went over to where Sam lay and pushed her new feline friend into her face. "Sam and Adrian sitting in a tree. K.I.S.S..."

"Don't be gross! Ugh!" Sam bolted up pushing the poor cat out of Karen's hand and into the air. Luckily he was a cat, and with a dramatic twist, he landed safely on his four paws - a little shaken but not stirred. Karen ran after him.

"I think we should go. Whatever silly plans they are

cooking up it's best we have nothing to do with them." I agreed and we all headed back to the main road.

5

HOME SWEET HOME

I turned the latch in my front door only to have my arm almost yanked off as my older sister pulled it open as she stormed out. My father followed close behind.

"I am warning you, Susannah Ward. If you see that boy again I will get the police onto him. He is trouble. Mark my words young lady. Come back in here right now!"

Susannah paused at the end of the path by the gate and turned defiantly.

"That's rich coming from you! How dare you tell me how to live my life when all the island knows what you get up to at the manor with your *friends*."

I had no idea what Susannah was talking about but my father softened slightly.

"Princess, please come back to the house. We can talk."

"I don't want to talk. I want to feel. I want to know joy. I want to make love. I want Trevor. And you can't stop me."

My father walked slowly down the path. His arms

outstretched. When he reached my now hysterically sobbing sister he pulled her towards him. They held each other. Then he pulled back and his face darkened.

"Did that little bastard make you do stuff with him? That's illegal, baby."

Susannah broke free.

"Is that what you think of me? I'm not stupid and he respects me which, it seems, is a lot more than you do. Don't follow me."

She walked off.

My father turned back to the house.

"What are you looking at? Haven't you got any homework? Get inside this minute!"

His voice wasn't angry though. It quivered. I rarely saw my father cry.

My mother, though, was often sad at bedtime.

Rosie was waiting for me at the bottom of the hall stairs.

"Will you play dolls with me?"

"Of course."

We went into the lounge and I closed the door to try to block off my parents' raised voices. Their row didn't last long. There was a bang, which sounded like one of them had hit the kitchen table and then the front door slammed. Heavy foot-steps crunched their way down the pebble path. The metal gate creaked open. Then silence.

"I like Daisy best. Her hair is so pretty. You have her friend, Havoc, she's like a boy. She has short red hair and a catsuit and guns. She is really cool but I like Daisy best. Look Mummy bought her a new dress. It's all sparkly like a rainbow. Is Zuzu in trouble?"

Rosie was never able to say Susannah's name properly.

"No, little sis. She will be okay. She just wants to play with the boys, like Havoc. She wants adventure."

"Boys are nasty. Bobby McGuire pulled my pigtails at school today. I don't like Bobby McGuire.

"Well, in that case. I don't like him either."

6

THE UNVEILING

"Psst! Where were you guys Friday after school? We waited at the graveyard for ages."

"Friday at five o'clock. What and miss Cracker-jack?" Jonathan replied in an overly exaggerated mocking voice. "Gotcha!" The boys laughed.

"Brooker, Little and Ward! Silence. We are in the house of God. There will be no more talking in the aisles. Have I made myself clear?"

"Yes, Mr Leybourne." We answered in unison.

"Right. Well, we are all gathered here today for a very special assembly. I will hand you over to Reverend Weeks." Mr Leybourne scowled at us all as he took his seat on the altar.

Reverend Weeks, an unremarkable man, was a new curate in the parish. I only saw him at school events like this as my family were not churchgoers. In fact, it felt quite strange sitting here. The pews were cold and hard. Everything was. The walls. The stone-flagged floor. Behind the altar though was a beautiful stained glass window with the image of St. Bridget holding a book and a staff topped with a lamp of fire. An ever-lasting flame. Wisdom and light, I thought. The light from June's rising sun shone through the coloured glass. I found it quite magical.

Next up after Reverend Weeks was Clifford Reid. He smiled broadly at someone behind us so I turned to see my aunt Cynthia standing right at the back of the church, leaning casually against a pillar. I caught her eye and she smiled and waved her hand indicating that I should keep my eyes facing front. Clifford was explaining his inspiration for the piece, still covered in a blue sheet beside him.

"I wanted to capture something uniquely British. Harking to the past, not of our distant empire of jingoism and colo-nialism but more of middle England. Cricket on the village green. Fish and chips walking along the pier of a seaside town. 'Kiss-me-quick' hats and saucy postcards. Tamed rose bushes and afternoon tea. Not Shakespeare or Jane Austen but Coro-nation Street and Carry-on. Not fox hunting but whippet racing. The Queen is the queen of us all. She may have her large estates with Inigo Jones landscapes but we, the common man, or woman, have our neatly manicured lawns and orna-mental fish ponds. These are our castles and our guardsmen!"

With a flourish, Clifford pinched the pointed corner of the sheet and pulled it off to reveal a three-foot-high garden gnome!

There was a gasp from everyone present.

A gnome! A garden gnome. A garden gnome wearing Union Jack trousers and a white t-shirt saying 'I love QEII'. On his head a black bowler hat and in his hand a pint of beer.

There was an awkward silence until one solitary clap began from the back of the church. I knew it was my aunt but I was too embarrassed to look around. My friends went to join in but I pushed their hands down. Couldn't they read a room?

The school secretary and parish organist, Mrs Cummings stood up and turned to Reverend Weeks and Clifford Reid.

"You cannot be serious! This … thing… is an abomination. We cannot present this to her gracious majesty. We will be a national laughing stock. What do you think we are? Those awful punk rockers! Boys, cover that monstrosity up at once." She pointed at two pupils sitting on the front pew and waved them to the altar. "Mr Leybourne dismiss the school at once. I shall speak to Reverend Cheeseman and Mr Forrest directly." And with that, she spun on her heels and marched out to the vestry.

I noticed that Clifford Reid was smirking, clearly amused by her outburst.

Adrian Little was smiling too. Mr Leybourne was hugely embarrassed and we hadn't had to do a thing.

7

THE PLOT THICKENS

"**O**h, Beverley! You should have seen her face! I thought old Alice Cummings was going to lay an egg. She has no sense of humour. A total killjoy. She's the Mary Whitehouse of Wesberrey. Thinks she's something because her daughter Rosemary married the Reynolds boy. Off on some oil rig in the North Sea. All she talks about is their lovely big house in Aberdeen. But he's still just an overpaid fisherman at the end of the day."

"Well, I think she has a point. Never before has a monarch of this land visited our island and you and your ridiculous boyfriend want to publicly humiliate us all."

Aunt Pamela had popped over to our house for afternoon tea and Cynthia was obviously catching her sisters up on the events of the morning.

"Here, Jess, darling. You tell them how funny it was. It put pompous Reverend Weeks in his place and that Mr

Leybourne. Man, we really do have a lot of starched shirts around here."

I joined my mother and aunts at the kitchen table. They were very close in age with barely three years between them. Mother always said she never understood how my grandmother had coped with three girls under three. My sisters and I, by comparison, were evenly spaced out three years apart. The upside for my mother though was that she and her siblings were extremely close though they couldn't have been more different in looks and temperament. Pamela was the eldest, solid, dependable with soft brown eyes and short brown hair which I now realised was styled in a similar way to the Queen's. My mother was the green-eyed middle child with a burnished auburn bob smoothly caught up in a pink headscarf. Cynthia wore her blonde locks in a soft beehive, the gentle fringe and loose strands framing her pale, blue eyes. Their looks were mirrored by me and my sisters. I took after Pamela, Susannah was a teenaged replica of Cynthia and Rosie, beautiful Rosie, was a lovely little miniature doll version of my mother.

"I think the gnome is quite funny. Maybe the Queen will laugh too."

"You see, " said Pamela, "even a child understands how inappropriate this is! Oh, and to think that everyone knows you and he are…"

"Are what? What, Pam, darling. Lovers? Go on say it! You know for a keeper of the Wells you have some pretty conservative, dare I even say Christian, views."

"Cynthia, how dare you question my allegiance. You know well how much I wanted to be the Godmother."

"Well, then darling, you shouldn't have married a cardigan and produced a male heir to inherit his model railway then."

"Take that back! Byron is a good man. He never says anything bad about you and heaven knows you give him plenty of ammunition."

"Sisters! Stop this now." My mother stood up and glared at her fighting siblings. "I think we all need to calm down. Cynthia, you are out of order. You both are. Apologise now and I will put on a fresh pot." I think I spotted that Mum was crying as she took the kettle to the sink. "So, let's hope all the other plans for the Queen's visit go more smoothly. I hear we are going to have a brass band and they are rigging up a huge PA system down on Stone Quay to play the National Anthem through when she arrives. Michael is using the one from the Somerstone estate. You know the one they use for the Bridewell Manor garden parties. Geoffrey has kindly agreed to let him use it. Michael has asked Susannah to help him. He thinks it will help."

The frustrating and equally wonderful thing about being a child is that adults forget you are there, especially if you appear to be busy with something else. On this occasion, I pulled out the latest copy of 'Look-In' magazine with DJ Ed Stewpot and a picture of Concorde on the cover. There was a poster of Tavares inside I thought Susannah might like. I had heard her listening to their music in her room. As I pretended to read about the latest episodes of 'The Tomorrow People' I was free to listen in on my aunts' conversation.

"Darling, Michael can't keep her locked in her room. I was the same. Do you remember, Pam, how Father used to stand guard outside my room all night listening out for any sign of movement? There were plenty of hours during the day when I could sneak off to see... Bev, help here, what was his name?"

"How do you expect either of us to remember? Poor Father. He tried so hard to keep us all safe after Mother died. It can't have been easy with three young girls."

"And you worried him sick. Always late, always in trouble. Then the boyfriends. That's why I married Byron. He reminded me of our father. Stoic, strong, dependable, caring. What you see as boring and dull is solid and virtuous."

"And Michael? Beverley, he has no right to judge Susannah, unless he is worried she is too much like him."

I lifted my eyes up slightly from my magazine. I didn't want them to notice I was listening. I failed.

"Sssh now, this isn't a conversation for tea time. What we need is cake to wash down all these sandwiches. Or, I got some of those 'Fudge' fingers Rosie is always singing the advert for. Jess, dear will you go and get her and call out to Susannah. I believe she's in her room."

8

GONE GNOME

"**D**id you take it? Answer me, Little. Did you take the gnome?"

" I swear, Sir. I don't know anything about it. We had footie practice at Scouts straight after school and then I was home. You can ask anyone, Sir."

Mr Leybourne released his grip from Adrian's collar and nudged him back to his seat. Straightening up, he adjusted his tie and turned to Miss Sykes.

"Mr Forrest has asked the police to interview the boys this afternoon. It has to be a stupid prank. We will get to the bottom of it. Make sure they are all outside his office at 2.30 pm sharp."

Miss Sykes almost curtsied in response. It seems that Clifford Reid's gnome had wandered off last night and was nowhere to be found. This was obviously a very serious matter if the police were involved.

"Children, erm, just take out the art things. I will be back in a few minutes."

"Where is Miss Sykes going? She looks very upset. It's only a garden gnome!" Karen whispered, as we both half-filled the jam jars with water to put out on the tables. "And why are they only interviewing the boys. Don't they think a girl could steal a stupid gnome? So much for Women's Lib, eh?"

We settled back at our table. I quite enjoyed 'free' art time. I hated being made to draw anything because it never looked right but just putting blobs of watercolour paint on absorbent paper and mixing the colours, that I enjoyed. My other favourite art lesson had been just before Christmas. We covered a sheet of paper with coloured crayons and covered it all again with black crayon. Then we scratched through to the colours beneath with the end of a compass. My drawing was very simple, a house with a door, windows, a chimney but it still looked beautiful as the colours shone through the dark. It reminded me of the stained glass window in St. Bridget's Abbey.

"I wish I had taken their bleeding gnome now. I'll get blamed for it anyway. The local cops hate us skater boys. It's not like we mess with traffic. There isn't any! Just a few horses and a couple of scooters. We don't cause any harm."

"Maybe that Clifford guy took it out to the cliff's edge, like Kunte Kinte and offered it up to the gods." Jonathan grabbed a doll from the dress-up area and stood on a chair with one foot on the table he raised the doll into the air, recreating a famous scene from the television series 'Roots'.

"And then he dropped it. Dashing its cement brains out on

the rocks beneath." William grabbed the doll and tossed it across the room.

"Both of you sit down, Do you want me to get in more trouble?"

"Miss Sykes is taking her time. Maybe she isn't feeling well. Some of us should check on her. Make sure she's okay." Sam suggested. Karen and I nodded. "You boys stay here and keep the class in order. Adrian if you are caught out in the corridors you will get the slipper again for sure."

As we snuck out into the hallway, Sam pulled Karen and me aside to share her idea about who had taken the gnome.

"Blaming the boys is too easy. It's too obvious. We were all ushered out of the church after Mrs Cummings left. The only people left with the gnome were Reverend Weeks, Mr Leybourne and Clifford Reid. Miss Sykes came back with us so it had to be one of them. Clifford Reid was proud of his work so it wouldn't be him, but both Reverend Weeks and Mr Leybourne were humiliated. Better to not present anything to the Queen than to give her something so offensive."

"It's just a gnome. I thought it was quite funny."

"Maybe, but what if the Queen wasn't amused. Can she still cut off people's heads?" I wondered.

"We don't even kill people for murder anymore. But I think their reputations would be badly hurt and both are ambitious men. Saying that, theft is a sin so I think that rules out the vicar so..."

"It must be Mr Leybourne. But why accuse Adrian Little and get the police involved."

"Jess, you are stupid sometimes. Adrian is just a patsy; a fall guy. Someone to take the rap for Mr Leybourne."

"Karen, you have been watching too much 'Starsky and Hutch'."

"No, Jess. I think Karen is right. Either Miss Sykes knows about it or she too has worked it out. She could be confronting him right now. She could be in real danger!"

"Over a gnome! He's not going to kill her. I think we should get back to class. You two have gone quite mad." I turned to go back to class.

Just then Miss Sykes emerged from the ladies' toilets. She looked very pale.

"What are you girls doing out of class, Come on with you. Let's get back."

"Are you okay Miss Sykes, you look a little peaky?"

"I will be fine, Sam. Thank you for asking. The milk in my cereal must have been a little off."

"Miss, we think it was Mr Leybourne who took the gnome and is setting Adrian Little up, Miss."

"Karen, don't be silly. There is no way Mr Leybourne did it. He was with me all evening."

9

CUMMINGS AND GOINGS

The boys had spent the lunch hour 'getting their stories' straight, which seemed a strange thing to do if they were innocent of kidnapping the gnome. Their story ran that after school they went straight to the church hall for scouts and football practice and then all went home. I felt that that alibi was fundamentally flawed as the hall had a door that led directly into the abbey and any one of them could have snuck through to take the gnome.

"Yes, but even if they did manage to go back how did they get it past the scoutmaster and everyone else without being seen?"

Sam made a good point. Karen looked pensive, she was brewing a brilliant idea.

"What if they didn't take it out? What if the gnome is just hidden somewhere else? No one would look elsewhere in the abbey. I mean you don't expect the gnome to wander off and hide, do you? You would assume it was stolen."

My head was full of thoughts, all falling over each other in a jumbled mess. Like Pooh, sat between my two friends I felt like a bear of very little brain. Who would hide it? Where could they hide it? Why would they hide it?

"Who discovered it was missing?" I asked.

"Mrs Cummings, I think. Then she told Mr Leybourne and he spoke to Mr Forrest who called the police. That's what I heard him telling Miss Sykes before he grabbed Adrian." Karen had been collecting the register off Miss Sykes to take to the office so she was closest to the conversation.

"So did any of them check the Abbey to see if it had been moved?" I asked. Karen shrugged her shoulders. Sam looked excited, she had an idea.

"I think we need to interrogate Mrs Cummings more. What was she doing in the Abbey? Why did she tell Mr Leybourne and not Reverend Weeks? Seems suspicious to me. I say one of us takes the afternoon's register to the office and gets some answers."

"But it's William's turn!" I protested.

"And all the boys are soon to be hauled up in front of the coppers so I think he will be wanting to avoid other authority figures, don't you?" Karen looked at me and folded her arms across her chest. "I think you should ask William if you can take his place. You have that innocent look. You can trick Mrs Cummings into squealing."

"Squealing?" I laughed "I'm not Kojak! But, I am willing to ask Mrs Cummings a few questions. She's a nice old lady. She looks like my grandmother with those huge glasses!"

"All old ladies look the same. Big-rimmed specs, tweed

skirts and crew neck sweaters. How *old* do you think she is? Mum says she is due to retire later this year."

"Don't let the little old lady look fool you. I think she's a criminal mastermind. Dad says many of these old ladies were in the army and stuff during the war. Maybe she was part of the French Resistance. She could easily dispose of a gnome if she took out Nazi soldiers with a piece of cheese wire." Karen moved her hand across her neck mimicking a knife blade.

"Karen, you have the most vivid imagination. But I will take the register and see what I can find out. Okay? Wesberrey Angels, we can solve this!" They nodded. I suddenly felt as green as Miss Sykes looked.

I took the register and made my way to the school office. It's a strange experience walking through the school corridors when everyone else is in class. Each class has a 'register', a large green book with the teacher's name written in black on the front cover. The cover itself is made of thick cardboard with a shiny plastic coating. Inside there is a column where all the pupils' names are written and then there are pages of boxes where our attendance is ticked off to cries of 'present' when the teacher calls out our names. If you don't answer a zero is marked against your name. The register is taken twice a day and afterwards, a nominated member of the class returns it to the school secretary. I really liked this job. The younger sets are sent out in pairs but I was now allowed to go out by myself. It was one of those duties that made me feel really grown up. I much preferred it to bringing in the milk for morning break (there was always pigeon poop on the silver bottle tops) or ringing the bell at the end of break time. I knew there would be a queue at the office so I took my time. I stopped to admire another class's noticeboard display of paper plate pictures of the Queen. Some of them were really good, though one had given her Majesty a lilac face and a blue crown. My delay to appreciate their art worked as there was no one else returning their registers when I got to the office.

" Come along Miss Ward, you're the last one."

"I'm sorry Mrs Cummings. Miss Sykes took a bit longer doing the register this afternoon. I don't think she's very well." I have no idea why I lied.

"Yes, well. Don't you go spreading rumours, Jessamy Ward. It takes two to tango."

I had no idea why Mrs Cummings was talking about dancing but I needed to get on with my mission.

"Terrible news about the gnome. Who discovered it was missing?"

"I suppose it was myself and Reverend Cheeseman. I was with him when he opened up this morning. He had been on the mainland till late and I wanted him to see the monstrosity that uncle of yours had created." I protested that Clifford Reid wasn't officially my uncle as he and my aunt were unmarried. "Ah, living in sin, eh? Well, no surprise there. We never see any of your family in church, do we?"

My family had always taught me that there were many ways to worship. Some did it at church and found God through hymns and statues but we were more inclined to observe our faith through marking the seasons and holding hands. I didn't think it was a problem. I understood the idea of 'sin'. It meant to do a bad thing. Though it was a phrase I had heard before, I couldn't see how my aunt was actively 'living in sin'. That would be a very silly thing to do.

"Mrs Cummings, may I ask? Did you look anywhere else for the gnome?"

"What a stupid question! It was left in front of the altar and then it was gone. It can't go for a walk by itself. Though, I'd like to thank whoever took the ugly thing. Maybe now we can forget the whole idea and get a little one from the Reception class to hand her Majesty a pretty posy instead."

I updated my friends when I got back to class. They were at the corner table doing French word puzzles.

"So it does sound like it was one of the boys, it certainly wasn't Mrs Cummings." Karen laid out a picture of a house, a mouse, a cat and a dog in front of me.

"Or Reverend Cheeseman, he was with her when they discovered it was gone and, according to Mrs Cummings, he hadn't been to see it in the evening." I looked bewildered at the French words before me.

"Right, and we know Mr Leybourne was with Miss Sykes. We have already ruled out Reverend Weeks." Karen impatiently took the card marked 'chien' and put it under the dog picture. Sam's mind was back on the boys.

"As the scouts were there playing football till dark, surely they would have spotted anyone acting suspiciously. Taking it out would have been very risky. And it's not dark until nine o'clock these days, so if the boys took it afterwards they would have been home really late. I think Adrian would have bragged to us about it by now. Or William would have fessed up. I think we need to get into the Abbey and take a good look. Karen is right. I think the gnome is still there."

Sam had the most curious look on her face. Forget French nouns, this was a puzzle she was very keen to crack, especially if it proved Adrian's innocence. I took a beat to consider my best friend's recently discovered interest in Adrian Little. Maybe Karen was right and Sam *fancied* him. I looked across the room. All three boys were sat on a separate table working on a Meccano set but were clearly nervous about seeing the headmaster. I suppose Adrian had a cheeky charm. If he was innocent, we had a duty to help him prove it.

"I agree." I placed the word card 'chat' under a picture of a cat. "I don't think the boys know anything. But, how are we going to get a look inside the Abbey?"

"Ah, well that's easy. Mum cleans the church. We'll just offer to help her."

I had forgotten that Karen's mother was a cleaner. She worked in a number of the larger buildings on the island, including Bridewell Manor and the school. It was why Karen was often at mine for supper as her Mum was working. Sam joined us for company as she had no siblings.

The police took hours interviewing the boys and, though we were concerned to hear how they got on, we needed to leave to help Mrs Clark at the abbey. Fortunately, Miss Sykes told us not to worry, that she would look after their satchels and make sure they were alright. So, as soon as the school bell rang, the Wesberrey Angels dashed off on our first assignment.

Karen's Mum was quite a character. A chain-smoking peroxide blonde with her hair dragged up high on her head in a large ponytail. I was amazed that her bright red nail polish was largely unchipped given her occupation. She still had a trim figure, which was hidden beneath a pale blue polyester work coat with navy cuffs and collar. For comfort, she wore pink slippers on her stockinged feet. It was unusual for married women to work. Most of our mothers stayed at home during the day doing their own cleaning. Some had small little part-time jobs but Mrs Clark worked several jobs. Her husband had had a bad accident on a trawler shortly after Karen was born and lived off the 'dole'. I guessed Mrs Clark and my mother were about the same age but Karen's Mum looked much older. Her face wrinkled prematurely by the cigarettes and constant exposure to the sun. My Mum shied away from the fashion for sun-worshipping, I think she burned easily. Karen's Mum, in contrast, was always as brown as leather.

"It's so nice of you girls to help me this evening. With your assistance, I should get back in plenty of time to catch 'Crossroads'. But we must be quick. Here, I gave the place a thorough once over a few days ago, just needs a little dusting." Mrs Clark handed us each a shocking pink feather duster.

Sam gave Karen and me clear instructions to not leave any space unchecked and off we set to a different corner of the nave. We each worked our way up and down the aisles but there were very few places where you could hide a toddler-sized gnome in a bowler hat.

"It was last seen in front of the altar. It's three foot of concrete, right? They couldn't have moved it far?" Karen got down on her hands and knees and started to crawl around the chancel.

"What in the heavens are you doing, young lady!"

Karen found herself looking at the polished black shoes of Reverend Weeks. She tried to pick herself up and grabbed at his trouser legs to steady herself. Mrs Clark flew in to save her daughter, and herself, any further embarrassment.

"Vicar, I am terribly sorry. The girls offered to help me tonight. They have been very respectful. Well, up until now. Karen, what were you doing down there?"

Recovering her composure Karen took a deep breath.

"We were looking for the gnome!"

"Yes," offered Sam, "We figured that it is too heavy to have been moved far so it must still be here somewhere."

Reverend Weeks slumped to the floor and sat with his head in his hands on the altar steps.

"It's under the altar cloth."

"It's what?" Mrs Clark walked over to the altar and carefully lifted up the green fabric by one of the gold tassels that edged the bottom. A pair of painted Union Jack trousers appeared. "Oh my!" Mrs Clark dropped the cloth. "Will someone explain to me what is going on here?"

Sam went full Sabrina Duncan on us and explained how Reverend Weeks had been so mortified by the idea of presenting the Queen with the disrespectful gnome he hid it so that he could get rid of it permanently later on.

"Technically, it's not stealing," she added, "As the gnome is still here. And I suspect it is not classified as lying unless you deliberately mislead inquirers about its whereabouts. The moment we challenged you your conscience gave it up."

Reverend Weeks nodded and said he was sorry but there was no way he could allow the Queen to receive such a tasteless gift. He told us how he had wanted to take it to the vestry but it was much heavier than expected, so he left it under the altar cloth for safekeeping until he could come back with a wheelbarrow. In fact, the wheelbarrow was waiting at the north transept but when he saw Karen on the floor snooping around he got nervous.

"And I'd have gotten away with it, too, if it weren't for those meddling kids!" he laughed.

A vicar who watches 'Scooby-doo' can't be all bad, I thought.

10
─────

THEY THINK IT'S ALL OVER

T he day of the Queen's visit arrived. Union Jacks and red, white and blue bunting fluttered from every window and post. Flower boxes and lawn beds were filled with matching blooms. Children of all ages waved their homemade flags. The stage was set for the historic royal event. No reigning monarch had ever stepped foot on the Isle of Wesberrey and, though the royal yacht would spend longer docking safely into the harbour than her Majesty would actually spend on her walkabout, it was still very exciting.

Since the case of the missing gnome had been solved the parish council had met to discuss what to do with the artwork and, unsurprisingly, it was agreed to not present the gnome to the Queen. Instead, Mrs Cummings was given the honour of escorting a boy and a girl from the Reception class as they each presented her majesty with a bunch of local flowers and a stuffed toy cat in honour of our famous feline colony. She had picked their names out of a hat in front of the whole school at assembly the day before. As I glanced over to the makeshift dais where the presentation was due to take place I could just make out a resplendent Mrs Cummings, dressed immaculately in peacock blue with a hat to match. She stood as proud as the bird whose colours she wore.

I was positioned with the rest of Miss Sykes's class at the end of the walkabout path nearest to the speakers. My father had borrowed the PA system from Lord Somerstone and, as promised, had roped in my eldest sister to help. They both sat behind us on a raised platform under a cover of white tarpaulin to keep the equipment safe should the weather turn. The rest of us were exposed to the elements but so far the sky had stayed clear and the sun appeared to be cooperating.

Some of the locals had been queuing for hours. The wiser ones had brought folding garden chairs with them and tartan flasks of tea were being passed around. The local brass band was saving itself for the Queen's arrival so, to pass the time, recordings of classical records were being played over the loudspeaker. Roaring patriotic tunes like 'Land of Hope and Glory' and 'Jerusalem' filled the air.

The rows of school children were becoming more and more restless as time wore on so Mr Forrest agreed to my father playing some pop music to 'calm the troops' as we waited. An eclectic mix of songs by Abba, the Muppets and Stevie Wonder soon had the crowd singing along as the sun danced in and out from behind ever-darkening clouds.

Finally, HMS Britannia sailed into view. The brass band readied itself on the opposite end of the quay for their signal and everyone raised their flags. The yacht's gangplank slowly lowered itself down onto the stone jetty. Everyone took a deep breath.

Silence.

Then over the loudspeaker, the unmistakable sound of 'God Save The Queen' by the Sex Pistols!

The signal went up. The brass band started playing and drowned out the loudspeaker just in time to see Her Majesty, Queen Elizabeth II set a dainty court shoe out of the yacht to begin her descent.

Behind me, I could hear the angry voice of my father chastising my sister. Boy, Oh boy was she in trouble this time!

11

GROUNDED FOR LIFE

"Oh, I remember your father was so angry!" Mum laughed "But he soon saw the funny side of it. I think he was very lenient."

"C'mon, Grandma. Did he ground her for life?"

"Well, Freya, if he did that it obviously didn't work, as you are both a testimony to. No, he got her a job at the manor house, mucking out the horses. She had to be up there at dawn every day for a month. He wanted to make sure she learnt a valuable lesson. Every action has consequences."

I looked at my mother and back at my nieces. "Mum, I don't think that is a lesson Zuzu has ever learnt."

My mother smiled. "Hmm, well maybe you can know something is wrong but still do it. Maybe you decide that the possible consequences are worth it?"

"So," asked Freya, "What happened to the gnome?"

"I believe he went back to Clifford's workshop. I think it featured in some retrospective show a few years later when

Clifford was diagnosed with cancer. Sad end. Cynthia really loved him. He was a great talent."

"Well," said Clara popping a final slice of cake on her plate, "I think Wesberrey sounds a wonderful place and I can't wait to visit once you are firmly installed."

"I'll help you move in, Aunt Jess," offered Freya "Someone needs to protect you from all those cats."

Yes, I thought. Mental note to self. Stock up on antihistamines.

The End

A STRING OF PERILS

A Jessamy Ward Mystery
The Isle of Wesberrey Series
A Short Story

LE ROI

"Jess, will you marry me?"

"Your timing sucks. Are you serious?" I pulled the cooler door shut and sunk flat against the stainless steel shelves.

"Deadly." Lawrence crouched low at my feet.

"Hmm. Can I park that till we find a way out of here?"

"Of course," he whispered.

Metal utensils clattered and clanged in the hotel kitchen outside. I scanned the cold room for potential weapons. "Did you grab anything useful? Like a knife or something?"

Lawrence held up a ladle.

"I'll take that as a no, then." Through the circular peep-hole, a black-clothed figure reached for a meat cleaver. I slid down. "If we stay low, hopefully, he won't see us."

"Are we sure it's a man? Looked female to me. Teenage boy, maybe."

The gender of our pursuer didn't matter, given the situation. I scooted my behind to wedge it in as tight to the door and my beau as possible. "Lawrence, I'm sorry."

"What about?" He wrapped his arm around my shoulder and drew me closer.

"Ruining your romantic Halloween plans with my psychic crime-fighting nonsense."

"Ah, that? Don't worry, you can't help it. It's why I love you. Anyway, what's a cosy dinner at the top of the Eiffel Tower when we can spend a terrifying October evening cuddling in the hotel's freezer instead?"

"Where are all the staff?"

"Trick or treating?" he joked. "Don't worry, someone will be along soon, and then the thief will make a run for it."

"With the countess's jewels." I sighed.

Lawrence planted a comforting kiss on my left temple. "You can't win them all."

The door to the cooler rattled. We pressed our bodies against it. *This is it. This is how it ends.*

"Hé, toi là-bas! Sors de la cuisine avant que Monsieur Renard ne te trouve."

Saved by the bellboy!

"So, Monsieur Pixley, you and Madame Ward chased the thief from Countess Von Schlagobers's suite and then hid in the freezer whilst they made their escape with over one million euros worth of jewellery."

"It's Reverend Ward, not madame. I am a vicar."

"Pardon, *Reverend* Ward."

"And, we didn't chase him. He chased us."

"Why would he do that?" The inspector snorted.

"Because we have something of his. Well, we had."

The inspector closed his notebook and waved my story on. "Go on, *Reverend.*"

"A memory stick."

The inspector tilted his head. Something was missing in translation. Lawrence, headmaster extraordinaire and techno-geek, proudly stepped forward to claim his prize.

"Une clé USB."

"Ah, mais oui, une clé USB. Où se trouve… Pardon, where is it now?"

"Well, you see… We were running for our lives," I explained.

"I put it somewhere safe." Lawrence flustered. "If we retrace our steps…"

This is embarrassing.

"We're not sure, inspector. But we can probably help you."

Lawrence caught the glint in my eye. So did the chief inspector.

"Merci, *Reverend* Ward. Monsieur Pixley. Let the police handle it from here."

Wedding proposals could wait. *We* had a memory stick to find.

SAFELY BACK IN our hotel suite, I slunk into a velvet bucket armchair and kicked off my heels. "How do other women wear these all day? I only had them on for a few hours and my feet are throbbing!" I massaged the cheesy lumps to pump much-needed blood to my toes. "And my ankles are so swollen! Getting old officially sucks."

Lawrence's pacing distracted me from my aching extremities. "Jess, I need to tell you something."

"Well, sit down first. You're paying a fortune for these rooms. Make the most of them."

Like a well-trained Afghan hound, he took point duty on the matching velvet sofa bed. When Lawrence announced two days ago he had arranged a surprise trip to Paris over the Halloween weekend, I would never have guessed he had booked a suite at the Le Roi.

The Le Roi was one of the oldest and most prestigious hotels in Paris. The rooms were enormous and must have cost my man a fair chunk of his headmaster's salary. I appreciated the gesture. The hotel was stunning, but I would have been more at home at a Budget Buster motel. *But don't tell him that.*

Lawrence, as always, behaved like the perfect gentleman and remained respectful of my desire to stay chaste until our wedding day. I was an Anglican vicar and took my beliefs seriously, even if my family's pagan heritage and my developing psychic powers constantly challenged them. Lawrence had slept on the sofa bed last night and would again tonight unless I took pity on him and swapped. That would be the Christian thing to do, but the mattress was so soft. He assured me this morning that he had slept like a log, even if his feet had been dangling off the end all night. *He's such a good liar.*

"I still have the USB stick. I didn't throw it away." He coughed.

"What? Then, why did you tell Inspector Clouseau that you did?"

"Because I didn't expect you to tell him. I panicked. Look, I think we can solve this." He slapped his thighs and sat back in triumph. "I know your head is already buzzing. You can't help yourself."

I swung my tired legs over the arm of the chair and made myself comfortable. "My spidey senses are telling me you know more about this than you are letting on. So, spill the beans, I'm all ears."

"My pleasure, my love, but first we need to make new plans for dinner. I'm starving. Chasing international jewel thieves is hungry work."

A QUICK CALL to the hotel manager and precious seats in the faux country club that is Le Roi's famous Hemingway Bar became available minutes later. Nothing was too much trouble for the valiant English couple who had chased after Countess Von Schlagobers's black pearls. My feet screamed their protest as I stuffed them back into their designer prisons. Now safely tucked underneath a green leather chair, I set them free once more. *So ladylike. Of course, Lawrence can't resist my charms!*

"Well, the fancy hot dogs are on their way. Time to talk!"

Lawrence leant in. The low seat forced him to bend his lanky frame. He resembled a praying mantis, and if not so earnest, would have been quite comical. *I love a man who can make me laugh.*

"Jess, remember yesterday when I booked you in for that

spa treatment?" *Honestly, with all the drama, I had forgotten all about it.*

"And it was a wonderful treat." I attempted a coy smile to show my appreciation. "This weekend has been unbelievably romantic. Well, except being trapped in a fridge, but—"

"Yes, well, I'll get to that in a minute. You see. I wasn't entirely honest. Whilst they wrapped you in mineral-rich clay, I slipped out for an appointment of my own."

"This tale had better not end in the red-light district." I joked.

Lawrence blanched. "I have never been to Pigalle Square!"

I laughed. "You know where it is, though?"

"Jess, I'm trying to be serious."

I mimed closing my mouth with an invisible zip.

Lawrence took a deep breath. "I was going to Bijoux."

"*The* Bijoux! The famous jewellers! What for?"

"To get your engagement ring!"

Before I could answer, the waiter appeared with our drinks. I grabbed my glass and took a deep gulp of whiskey and soda. *Well, we are in a bar named after Ernest Hemingway, surrounded by his memorabilia. It would be wrong to drink anything else.*

"From the Bijoux!" I choked back the amber liquid. "Ooh la la! Monsieur Pixley, you have such style."

"See, this is what I wanted to avoid. It's all a mess. I'm a mess! Why would you consider marrying me?"

With my glass-free hand, I stretched across to stroke his thigh. It was all I could reach. "Why would you think you had to bribe me with posh hotels and expensive rings? I already told you I would say yes. You could have proposed on Skegness

Pier and placed a doughnut ring on my finger. My answer would be the same."

"That's all fine and dandy," he huffed. "But I wanted Paris, dinner atop the Eiffel Tower, and a room at the Le Roi."

"Well, you managed two out of three. Where's the ring now?" I dangled my left hand above his knee.

"No, I want to do it properly. You'll have to wait."

I made a play of pretending to be insulted by his rejection, crossing my legs and kicking the coffee table just as our food arrived. The waiter expressed concern for my bruised shin, to which the two of us giggled like naughty children.

Unimpressed, he slid our food onto the offending table. "Bon appétit, Madame. Monsieur."

"I think we're lowering the tone." I snorted into my glass. "Now where were we? You were at Bijoux, buying me a ring, Solitaire? Diamond, right? How much did you spend?"

"Jess, look, what happened next is very important. I was standing at the counter beside a very strange character. He looked like that artist. What's his name? White hair. Sunglasses."

"Andy Warhol?"

"Yes, that's him. Anyway, he was very shifty. Kept looking around and sniffing. Well, you know I suffer with my allergies, so I took pity on him and offered him a fresh handkerchief. I tapped him on the shoulder and he had such a fright he dropped the paper bags he was holding and in the panic, mine went flying to the floor too. I apologised, of course, picked my bag up straight away and tried to help him with his purchases."

These overpriced mini hot dogs are delicious. "Go on."

"He was furious. I mean incandescent. But, he didn't say a word. Just grabbed the other bags and stormed out. The security guards were a little slow to open the door, and he just pushed past them. I ran after him to apologise again and you will never guess what he did next."

I pointed at my stuffed mouth and shrugged.

"He jumped on one of those e-scooters and took off like the clappers!"

I swallowed. That bizarre image needed a reply. "He must have been quite the sight."

"Yes, yes, he was. Anyway, when I got back here, you were still at the spa so I thought I would get the ring out and that's when I realised my mistake."

"Don't tell me you picked up the wrong bag! Lawrence!" I gasped.

"I know. It's like an episode from the Pink Panther. Instead of your ring, there was a brooch. Black pearls on a gold mount, with the initials V and S intertwined."

"V and S? Von Schlagobers!" I whispered through a mouthful of mustard and ketchup filling.

"Well, yes. I twigged that connection whilst we were waiting in the cold room. Maybe if I had realised before, I would have stopped you from making us visit her apartment on our way out to apologise. For nothing, I might add. You were only trying to help."

"Do you still have the brooch?" Thoughts were tumbling over my mind like a clown cavalcade.

"No. Bijoux is a few minutes away, and well, remember after breakfast I apologised for disappearing because I had a few work calls to make? Well, I sped back to the shop and was there when they opened. Fortunately, they had another ring in your size, so they just made the swap. Very trusting, really. I guess they figured Mr Warhol would realise the error and take the ring back at some point."

"And the USB?"

"Ah, well. Hmm…. You see, I forgot about that. It was underneath the brooch and, er, I know it's wrong, but curiosity got the better of me and I tried to open it. Very stupid, really. It was password protected, naturally."

I viewed my potential fiancé in a more critical light, and not without a disarming level of admiration. "And where is the USB now? I take it you forgot to return it to the shop."

He nodded. "It's still in my pocket, along with a spare hanky, a blue biro cap, and a handful of Murray mints."

"You must be the only man in the world to carry Murray mints. I hear most men prefer Werther's Originals these days."

WE ROUNDED off our late supper with some cognac. My natural tendency is to drink wine, so spirits go straight to my head, making me incredibly sleepy. I yawned like a hippo. Lawrence called for the bill.

"Non, monsieur. Votre la note est payée. Voyez, la dame en robe jaune."

Lawrence turned to check out the lady at the bar who had settled our account. "Yellow dress? Ah, yes. Er… Veuillez lui dire merci et l'inviter à se joindre à nous." My beau's mastery of French was very attractive, though I'm sure a native would take issue with his accent, which was very English home counties.

The waiter smirked as he bowed and backed away to complete his new task. "She paid our bill. She must work for the countess. I've invited her to join us." Lawrence explained.

"Who?" My limited French was struggling to keep up.

"The lady in the yellow dress."

Right on cue, a slender brunette, oozing Parisian style, with the straightest hair and blackest eyes I have ever seen, slinked over to join us. "Monsieur Pixley. Madame Ward. I hope you enjoyed your meal. When the countess heard that you had missed dinner and were in the Hemingway, she insisted I pay for everything. She is very grateful for your help."

Lawrence's cheeks flushed. He pulled across a chair for our pretty guest and sat back down with all the grace of a marionette. *I'm not normally jealous, but something about the glint in his eye is pushing all the wrong buttons.*

"But the thief got away?" I interjected.

"Oui, but…" the coal-eyed vixen stroked Lawrence's knee. "You were so brave, chasing him through the hotel, with no thought of your own safety."

My cheeks were on fire, and it wasn't a menopausal flash. Green steam formed in the furnace of my suspicious mind. This French minx was flirting with my soon-to-be fiancé. Time to assert my prior claim over the gangly hero.

"I chased them away too, you know." *Nothing petulant about that statement.* "Thank you for your hospitality, but we need to get to bed soon. I'm sure you understand."

I navigated my shoes back onto my engorged feet. They

were as miserable as the rest of me. As my creaking body rose from the chair, the leather seat beneath me sighed with relief. *Really? A flatulent chair!* It was time to leave. I coughed to get Lawrence's attention.

"Sorry, my sweet. Yes, it is late, and it's been quite a day. Please excuse us, miss?" He took the stunning brunette's hand.

Call me Chloé." The coquettish tilt of her head was almost clichéd. *Lawrence wouldn't fall for that, surely?*

"Chloé, what a beautiful name. It suits you."

It what now?

"Come, my love. I am sure *Chloé* here needs to be some-where else. We have imposed on her time too much already."

"Please, before you go. The countess would like you to join her for breakfast. She has a table reserved in the Café Vendôme. I hope eight is not too early?"

CAFÉ VENDÔME

"Jess, what is wrong with you? I've never seen you like this." Lawrence pressed the button for our floor. As the metal door closed, he slipped a playful arm around my waist and nuzzled his face into the nape of my neck. "I quite like it though."

"I don't know what you mean." *Embarrassed to say, I know exactly what he means.* "We can send our apologies to breakfast, right?"

"Not if you want to solve this mystery," he teased. "Don't you think it's suspicious that the countess wants to meet us again? She was pretty weird about your psychic stuff earlier. So much so that you felt a burning desire to go back again and apologise for upsetting her. But now we are her new best friends, even though we didn't prevent the theft. Seems strange to me."

Lawrence backed out of the lift and guided me down the corridor, stealing kisses along the way. All green-eyed thoughts of Chloé dissipated in the reality of his loving embrace. Whilst I believed in no sex before marriage, I wanted to show Lawrence how serious I was about taking the next step. It was time for a moment of grand passion. *After all, we are in France!*

I reached up on tippy toes and planted a whopping big kiss on his gorgeous lips, pushing him back into the door of our suite. Instead of standing firm, the door opened, throwing us both into the lounge. Lawrence scooped me up with the skill of an experienced figure skater and twirled us around to face the room.

Someone had trashed it.

Our orderly love nest resembled a teenage boy's bedroom. Fortunately, without the smell. Drawers left hanging. Wardrobe doors open-mouthed. And the carefully hung clothes from within them festooned the bed, tables, and floor. I wanted to cry, but my tears were too shocked to come out.

Lawrence pulled the USB out of his pocket. "Do you think they were looking for this?"

"Probably." I panted. The shock of seeing our little home from home in such disarray winded me. "But how would they know it could be here? Did you give Bijoux your room number?"

"I don't think so. I might have mentioned I was staying at Le Roi."

"And there are probably not that many blond Englishmen over six foot two staying here. You would have been easy to find. They took a risk coming here at this hour unless they knew we were in the bar. Then again, if the countess knew we were there, anyone could have found out. We have to call the police."

As NOTHING APPEARED to be taken, there was little the police could do except to take our statements. It was a hotel room, fingerprints were hardly conclusive leads. The inspector was more interested in checking the CCTV footage and was quick to move the investigation on. He agreed the perpetrator was probably looking for the USB stick. Which Lawrence, again, failed to mention was in his pocket!

The hotel moved us into a different suite, conveniently or suspiciously, on the same floor as the countess. I was too tired to question Lawrence's rationale for withholding evidence but decided a good night's sleep might help improve his decision-making skills. I volunteered to take my turn on the sofa bed and let him have the king in the main bedroom.

Despite the surprising comfort of the foldout mattress, I struggled to get any rest. My mind milled over and over the events of the day. Computing the facts and the fiction until my head throbbed. My future fiancé was a dark horse capable of creative deception. Even if his intentions were honourable, his actions were misleading. Sneaking out to buy me an expensive engagement ring was cute, but withholding vital information from the police was worrying.

Jess, listen to yourself! How many times have you not told the police back home about an important clue when you had a hunch?

And it was one of my hunches that brought us into the countess's world yesterday afternoon. When Lawrence left me alone at breakfast to 'make some phone calls', an elderly American lady, who I was to learn was Countess Marta Von Schlagobers, invited me to join her at her table. The countess had overheard our English accents and wanted to chat in her native tongue. Her family had emigrated to the United States when Hitler came to power in such a rush that all they had taken with them were her famous jewels and their hereditary titles.

"Can you believe I have travelled the world many times over, but I have never set foot in the fatherland?" The countess dropped four white cubes in her coffee. "I see your disapproval. Sugar is a terrible vice, but at my age, who cares?"

She stirred the lumps until they dissolved. "We are doing a grand tour. Starting here in Paris and ending in Istanbul. I want to do it all before I die. Budapest. Venice. I will visit the old country next. My mother was pregnant with me when they left Germany. Can you imagine how terrifying that journey must have been? And look at us now, enjoying peace and prosperity."

"You say 'we'? Are you travelling with other members of your family?"

The countess was a formidable woman, elegantly dressed in flowing lime green chiffon which skimmed her thin, tanned figure. I felt more dumpy than usual in my comfy sweats, ready for a day of sightseeing.

"I am here with my partner, Jeremy, and my assistant. She is French, so Paris had to be our first stop."

"And they aren't joining you for breakfast?"

"No, Jeremy is in the pool and, to be honest, I have no idea where my assistant is. She busies herself with a thousand errands a day. I expect she will report back after lunch. I thought I would take a taxi to the Louvre this morning. You and your husband can share with me if you wish?"

"Oh, Lawrence is not my husband." *Why did I have to say that?* "He has today all planned out. I believe he has bought tickets for the riverboat tour down the Seine."

"In October? Rather you than me, my dear. Oh, look, I think your lover has returned." I turned towards the door. Lawrence waved across, flushed and slightly out of breath. "He seems keen to get on. Well, off you trot, my dear." Her manicured fingers tapped the back of my hand.

It was brief, like the static shock you sometimes get walking across a nylon carpet, but a worrying image flashed behind my eyes. A dart of lime green. A scream. Someone wailing, then silence. Crimson liquid seeped across the scene in its dying moments. Like a montage in a thriller movie trailer, suggesting menace but giving away none of its secrets.

I wanted to say something there and then, but how could I explain I had the unwelcome gift of second sight. A sixth sense passed down through the female line of my family. I had only learned about it myself this past year. Reconciling this knowl-edge with my Christian beliefs was bad enough. It was one thing to discuss this with friends and family back home on the Isle of Wesberrey, but in Paris with a total stranger? And what would I say? For all I knew, her beautiful dress might be on course for a collision with a glass of Merlot over dinner.

I bid my goodbyes and skipped out of the restaurant as quickly as possible. Of course, the guilt travelled with me all over Paris. The scream replayed itself over and over in my head until I begged Lawrence to take me back to the hotel.

The countess received news of my premonition graciously, but it had unnerved her. Marta's left eye twitched. The gilt-edged cup she held rattled as she placed it back on its matching saucer. Her breath quickened. But the words she used to dismiss my concerns were resolute and calm. She assuaged my fears by promising me she had planned to change for dinner anyway and would make sure that she packed away the lime green dress, breaking whatever curse she was under.

I had made quite the spectacle of myself.

In fact, I had felt so embarrassed by the whole crazy conversation that, even though we were already running late for our date with the Eiffel Tower, I insisted we swing back to the countess's suite to apologise. However, instead of the countess, we found a figure dressed in black, with a mask covering their face, rifling through her belongings.

Lawrence sounded the alarm. The masked ninja went for him with the knife they had been using to slice open the soft furnishings. I grabbed an ornament and swiped the burglar across their shoulder blades, though I was aiming for their head. Taking advantage of my poor aim, the dazed villain grabbed at the jewels on the table, stuffed them into their pockets and dashed into the hallway.

Stupidly, we gave chase.

At some point, the pursuers became the pursued, and we ended up hiding in the chiller. It was all a bit of a blur, to be honest. When Lawrence first mentioned the USB in the cooler, I assumed the fiend had dropped it. I didn't know Lawrence had it the whole time.

I MUST HAVE FALLEN asleep at some point because my next memory was waking up to Lawrence stroking stray hairs off my face.

"What time is it?"

"Seven-thirty. You looked so beautiful, I didn't want to disturb you."

"Do you lie about everything?" I protested as I wiped the drool from my lips. "Here, help me get up." Lawrence stood, reached down a hand, and yanked my weary frame forward. "Don't know why I ache so much. Getting old, I guess."

"Stress." Lawrence offered me a coffee. "I think we should send our apologies to the countess. We have until noon to take breakfast."

"No, let me swig this down. One question. Why didn't you tell the police about the USB?"

"I don't know. Maybe your psychic stuff is rubbing off on me. I just have a feeling it's important."

"Given they trashed our room for it, I don't think you need paranormal powers to work that out." I joked.

"Maybe not." He planted a sneaky kiss. "Mmm, coffee breath. Make sure you brush your teeth."

CAFÉ VENDÔME, with its green painted iron skeleton and glass walls and ceiling, dazzled in the Saturday morning sunlight. Today was All Hallows' Eve, but there were no signs of any Halloween decorations. Everything was just as refined as it had been at breakfast the day before. The maître d' showed us to the countess's table.

"Thank you both so much for accepting my invitation. I so enjoyed our conversations yesterday, but I fear you were holding out on me, *Reverend* Ward? You failed to tell me you were a priest! And one that has spooky premonitions, too. You're like an onion. So many layers. Fascinating. I was telling Jeremy here, and he missed his morning exercise just to meet you."

"I'm honoured."

Jeremy leapt to his feet to pull out my chair. He was not like I expected, though I will be honest I had not given him much thought. Jeremy was several decades her junior, though it was hard to place his age with any certainty. Super snug white chinos and a pink polo shirt hugged his boyish frame. Under the luminous apricot tan, he still wore the freckled face of youth. He may have been in his mid to late thirties at a push.

My surprise at the age gap must have shown in my expression, despite my intention to remain neutral. "My, my, Jeremy, I think we have scandalised the vicar!" The countess laughed. "Jeremy is my business partner! I run a little import and export business. Well, let's be honest, Jeremy does. He's my best friend and the closest thing I have to family."

"I'm sorry. As they say, never assume, it makes an ass out of you and me." I looked to Lawrence for help, but he was too busy scanning the menu to appreciate my dilemma.

"Marta, you were right. She really is too sweet!" Jeremy clapped. "Let's order. Chloé will be here soon, and we have a lot of meetings lined up today."

"Oh, be a sweetie and do them all without me? You don't need me there, and we have the ballet tonight. I have to pace myself." The countess didn't wait for an answer. I imagined she had trained Jeremy not to argue. Marta refocused the spotlight on me. "I understand the thief attacked your room last night as well. One would think we would be safe at Le Roi."

Lawrence looked up over the menu that, until then, had taken his full attention. "I'm sure it was the same person. I think they are looking for something."

Jeremy eyed us both up and down. "No offence, but what could you have they would want?"

"Well, they were clearly looking for something when they raided your suite earlier that evening. We disturbed them. Maybe they thought we had taken it. Whatever it was." Lawrence paused briefly to give the waitress his order. Eggs Benedict on sourdough toast.

"Countess Von—"

"Please, we are friends now. Call me Marta."

"Marta, yes. I was wondering exactly what did the thief take?"

The countess took a thoughtful sip of orange juice. "Only my black pearls. They left the emeralds and the diamonds, though they were in the safe. Why they cut up the cushions, I don't know. Just seems like senseless destruction to me. Must be some desperate soul trying to feed his starving wife and children. I just wish he had taken the emeralds. They may be worth thousands of dollars, but they are terribly tacky. I would sell them but for their sentimental value. The pearls were my grandmother's. A gift from a Prussian prince."

Marta's eyes brimmed with tears. She bristled, and with a deep, restoring breath, changed the subject. "The hotel manager has been very understanding."

"They moved us to a new room." I offered.

Jeremy stirred cream into his coffee. "Oh, they offered to move Marta too, but she's as tough as nails. Aren't you, dear? You said the last person to hound you out of your home was Adolf, and you don't bow down to criminals."

"Very admirable. May I ask how much would you say they are worth?" Lawrence was obviously itching to know more about the stolen jewels.

"Valuations are so vulgar." The countess waved a dismissive hand. "But interestingly, Jeremy had just had them appraised at Bijoux for me."

"Oh." Lawrence's interest piqued, he leaned in to drive on his interrogation. "When was this?"

Jeremy shifted in his seat. It may have been nerves or the tightness of his trousers. "I took them in when we first arrived, so what day is it today? Saturday?"

"Yes, the thirty-first. Halloween."

"Ah, yes. So that would have been on Thursday. I went to collect them Friday morning."

"You went to get them in the morning?" Lawrence kicked me under the table. I realised the significance of his question. If Jeremy had picked up Marta's pearls earlier in the day, then they couldn't have been the same ones that Lawrence had picked up by mistake, and the USB belonged to someone else. Logistics aside, Jeremy looked nothing like Andy Warhol.

Lawrence's hunch was leading us nowhere. His confidence deflated. My heart twinged with sympathy for my beau. Then I clocked his reaction to Chloé sauntering towards the table, and my compassion took a dramatic nosedive.

Jealous? Who me?

"Ah, Monsieur Pixley. *Reverend* Ward. Excusez-moi. Marta, we have an appointment with the American ambassador in an hour. Have you eaten yet?"

"Oh, Chloé, you worry so. The food will be here soon. We've plenty of time. Jeremy ordered for you. Sit down and relax."

Much to my annoyance, Chloé did as instructed and pulled up a chair. Lawrence's spirit lifted too much for comfort.

Jess, you are a disgrace to your clerical collar! Talk to the beautiful girl.

"So, Chloé. Marta was telling me yesterday that you are French. Do you have family in Paris?"

"Oui, my brother lives here." A delicate pink blush flooded her cheeks. I could feel Lawrence's protective testosterone rising. "But we don't talk anymore. It is sad, but our lives have taken different paths." She bit her lower lip and sniffed back tears.

The countess stretched across the table and cupped her assistant's hand in hers. "Poor Chloé. We don't talk about her brother, Anton. He was a hero. A brave firefighter until ... until his accident. Then he got hooked on painkillers and other substances. It was a slippery slope. He is now a husk of his former self. Chloé did everything she could to help him. You know, he even stole from their mother to feed his drug habit. It's very tragic."

All my spiteful thoughts shamefully sought refuge in the dark recesses of my mind. "I am so sorry. I didn't mean to upset you."

"C'est d'accord." Chloé's coal eyes dimmed. Her smooth

complexion paled. "Ah, the food is here. We should eat more and talk less. Yes?"

We all tucked into our different choices and marvelled at the myriad ways one can cook eggs. Florentine, Benedict, scrambled, poached with salmon or ham, on toasted muffins or sourdough bread. Desperate to change the mood, I asked if anyone could recommend where we should go in Paris for Halloween.

Chloé quickly closed down that line of conversation. "We do not celebrate Halloween here. It is an American invention. We save ourselves for La Toussaint - the feast of All Saints. As a member of the clergy, you must observe that too? Not this commercial pagan nonsense."

Suitably chagrined, I simply nodded in response.

Lawrence rode in to rescue the shreds of dignity I had left. "It is a national holiday, I understand. It's a shame we have to leave in the morning for the airport. Tonight is our last night."

"Your last night! My dears, you must come to the ballet. I have a box at the Palais Garnier. You cannot deny me. Just for the famous chandelier alone. Who knows, perhaps we shall see the Phantom of the Opera himself."

Lawrence morphed into an excited nine-year-old. "Is it true there is a lake beneath it? I have always wanted to see that. Jess, please say yes. I have only seen pictures of the auditorium online."

How can I say no?

~

TODAY'S EXCURSION was to the Sacré-Cœur Basilica. The thought of climbing the hills in Montmartre and then the three hundred steps to the church itself was daunting. I wasn't sure my already sore feet and aching calves would thank me afterwards.

"Maybe the concierge could get us a taxi? We could walk back down."

"Jess, it's a glorious day today. Do you really want to spend it in traffic? We can take the metro and walk up." Lawrence thrust a map in front of me. "Look, it's not far."

"I've checked TripAdvisor, and it's not for the faint-hearted. And how is being sardined underground better than riding around in style above ground? At least we will see the city that way."

As we stood there arguing in the foyer, Jeremy and Chloé came out of the lift. They were deep in conversation and didn't notice us, or if they had, they did a great job of ignoring us. Their body language was a tad more intimate than I expected. When they entered the revolving doors, I could swear Jeremy slipped his arm around her waist.

"Did you see that?"

"No. What?"

"Come, quickly." I grabbed Lawrence's hand and rushed towards the entrance, just in time to spot the couple hail a cab. Skipping down the stairs after them, I dragged Lawrence behind me.

"Taxi!" A black Renault saloon pulled up to the curb. "Lawrence, can you ask him to follow that cab?" I shouted back as I dived into the back seat.

"Er, suivez ce taxi !" Lawrence mumbled as he folded

himself into the seat beside me. After some frantic pointing and expressive gesturing, we were soon on the trail of our prey. "Jess, if I knew you wanted to grab a cab this much—"

"Sssh, we are following Jeremy and Chloé. Where do you think they are heading?" We drove past the Jardin des Tuileries, along the Place de la Concorde and pulled in alongside an impressive sandstone wall housing an ornate cast-iron fence, behind which stood an imposing four-storey mansion in the same cream stone, with a balustrade running the full length of the roof. Above the huge wooden door flew the 'Stars and Stripes'. It was the American embassy. "Ah, Chloé said they had an appointment with the ambassador."

Lawrence squeezed my thigh. "Come now, it was a gamble. Let's carry on with our day as planned." He leaned forward and tapped the driver on the shoulder. "S'il vous plaît, montez au Sacré Coeur, merci."

"I'm sorry. I don't know what came over me. My gut is telling me that Chloé is up to something."

"Are you sure you're not jealous? I mean, I'm flattered, but she's half my age!"

"So, you *do* find her attractive. I knew it." My inner toddler pouted her displeasure. I pretended to focus my mind on the passing Parisian architecture. Lawrence's smugness filled the car. I didn't need to look to register the knowing smirk on his face.

The view from the basilica was exceptional and well worth the cab fare to enjoy it without sacrificing whatever goodwill my feet still afforded me. We took our time to stroll down. The autumnal sun warmed the cobble streets and all around the sounds and smells of bustling cafes filled the area. Scooters whizzed past, threatening the life and limbs of inattentive tourists checking their maps or reading a blue enamel street sign.

We stopped for lunch at a cute little corner cafe that screamed bohemian artist with its faded painted shutters and mismatched tables and chairs. As I tucked into a toasted sandwich, I imagined sitting here with Van Gogh, Toulouse-Lautrec, or Degas.

I closed my eyes to visualise nimble ballerinas warming up for a class, a sea of peaches and cream. "Do we know what the ballet is tonight?" I asked.

Lawrence swiped open his phone, and his thumbs danced across the screen. "It's a contemporary production that, and I quote, examines the mutability of life, the constant flux between birth and death and the necessity of pain to transition and grow."

"Wow, sounds delightful!" I laughed. "Are you going to give the police the USB when we get back? We have no more clues to pursue."

"We don't, but we have you. What if you do that thing you do with the memory stick? I can't help but think everything is connected. We just don't know how, yet. You felt the countess was in danger. Perhaps she still is. We can't just walk away."

I breathed a heavy sigh and held out my palm expectantly. "You win, hand it over." Lawrence placed the USB in my hand, and I closed my eyes again.

It was Halloween, after all. The day when the veil between this world and the next is at its thinnest. Back home, children dress in fancy costumes ready to tour the neighbourhood in search of candy. Though we were in one of the most beautiful cities in the world, part of me missed that homely tradition.

Chloé was right. Trick or treating is a recent American import and not something I did as a child. Instead, my mind threw up distant memories of Samhain celebrations from my past. Bobbing for apples and other familial rites that I had long forgotten. Perhaps I could use the power of the day to channel further insights... perhaps.

What I had learnt over the past year was that this psychic stuff was not an exact science. You had to be patient, and there were no guarantees. It didn't help that I hadn't a clue what I was hoping to find.

The small plastic dongle warmed in my hand. My head spun, and I was soon to regret having extra cheese in my toasty. A fatty lump gathered at the back of my throat, causing me to gag. I swallowed hard. Breathing deep in through my nostrils, my head rocked back and a white light engulfed me. I emerged on a wooden stage, staring out into a sea of red velvet. Someone was behind me. I could feel their hot breath on my neck. I turned. A slim black figure with a mask lunged towards me. I stumbled.

"Jess? Wake up!"

I pried open my eyelids, unsure of where I was. Lawrence was fanning me with a copy of the bistro's menu.

"Someone is in danger. At the ballet. I'm sure. The thief will be at the Palais Garnier tonight."

OPÉRA GARNIER

We took the metro back and arrived at the hotel with enough time for a quick nap before heading off to the theatre. Before resting my head on the voluminous white pillows, I took a beat to put in a brief prayer to the Boss. I often had to remind myself these days that my calling is to the church first and my family's pagan heritage second.

My aunts assured me that one did not negate the other, that I could serve both in equal measure. But whilst I had inherited the gifts, I did not share their allegiance to the goddess. I was a child of God, and it was to him I turned for support each day.

My prayer ended. I lay down to rest. *Who is going to believe a psychic priest? And what was I going to tell them, anyway?* My restless mind buffeted the events of the past few days around like a fishing fleet off a stormy Cornish headland. If only I could find the light to guide them safely home. I had no clues, only visions and Lawrence's hunches to go on. We had the USB, and that was important, somehow. But without the password to decode it, there was no way we could use it to identify the thief.

But we could use it to draw them out…

I jumped out of the bed and ran towards the lounge. Lawrence was fiddling with a small blue velvet box, which he snapped shut and put behind his back as soon as he heard me approach.

"I thought you were taking a nap?"

"I thought so too, but I have an idea. We need to take a trip to Bijoux."

Ten minutes later we were waiting at the counter of the luxury jewellers. "Do you remember who was serving Mr Warhol that day?" I whispered.

Lawrence looked around. "I can't see him."

"Do you remember his name?"

"Well, no, as he wasn't serving me. But, hold on, he was here when I returned the brooch."

I pulled Lawrence to the far wall, ostensibly to look at the necklaces on display in the glass cabinet. "Close your eyes and describe him."

"Average height, perhaps a little on the short side. It's so hard for me to gauge as I tower over everyone. Dark, slim build. His eyes were… I can't see his eyes, sorry. He wore gloves. White gloves. I guess for handling the jewellery."

I snaked my arm around his back. "Take a deep breath and try again." Whilst Lawrence went deeper into his memory, I tried to read his mind. I had never done this before. I wasn't even sure it was possible.

"Anton!" Lawrence kissed me excitedly on the lips. "The name on his badge was Anton!"

We asked a member of staff if Anton was available, only to find that he was on a break, but we could leave a message.

"What should we write?" I asked.

"How about we've got what you want, meet us at the Palais Garnier?"

"Why there?" Images from my bizarre premonitions flipped my stomach.

Lawrence brushed my hair behind my ear and leaned in so close his breath tickled me. "Because we need to lay a trap for Andy Warhol."

IT WAS time to share what we knew with the police. Once safely back in our hotel room, Lawrence called the inspector and explained that he had 'found' the memory stick and outlined our suspicions. Reluctantly, the inspector agreed to go along with our plan to unmask Le Roi's cat burglar at the theatre that evening.

We had a few minutes spare to get dressed. "So who's your primary suspect?" I adjusted Lawrence's bow tie and turned around, pointing for his help with the zip on my dress.

"Jeremy. He took the jewels into Bijoux to be appraised. I think he struck a deal with Anton to create replicas of the gems, and then he would sell the originals. Perhaps the USB contains details of potential buyers. He returned later in disguise to collect the fakes and the memory stick."

"Hmm, I agree the jewels you saw were probably copies, and the duplicates made whilst at the jewellers'."

Adjusting my shoulder straps, I searched the room for my shoes. *I hate dressing up to go out. So many bits to coordinate.* I always feel more at home dressed in a simple black shirt and trouser combination with a white dog-collar accent at the neck. *But when in Rome, sorry, Paris.*

"But why would Jeremy need to go back a second time to collect the fakes? And why the Andy Warhol disguise?"

"The disguise is obvious, to distract witnesses." Lawrence checked himself over in the mirror. "I mean, who would believe they saw Andy Warhol on an e-scooter stealing jewellery from Bijoux?"

"I believed you. But be honest, though you thought it weird, you didn't suspect anything criminal was taking place. I imagine that was the idea. So, yes, distraction. But why the need to trick and confuse people?"

Lawrence slumped in the armchair after wrestling with his tan brogues. "To throw suspicion elsewhere. Do you think Warhol is the burglar? I would say they were a similar height and build."

"No, I think they are two separate people, but they are in it together. For what it's worth, my money is on your girlfriend, Chloé."

"And what evidence do you have for that? Above pure jealousy." Lawrence sniffed.

"Anton is her brother," I added, smugly. "And what better disguise for a woman than to dress as a man?"

∼

WE JOINED the countess and her party, and together we strolled along busy Parisian roads to the Palais Garnier. It was a pleasant ten-minute walk passing shops and restaurants as French life transitioned from work to pleasure. The traffic provided a heady backing track of lights and impatient horns.

Everyone was busy going somewhere. Some were even in Halloween costumes, mainly young adults, presumably on their way to a themed party or nightclub. Marta and I made pleasant small talk about the various sights and sounds along our journey. Lawrence brought up the rear, talking to Jeremy about reviews of the ballet he had read online.

Chloé remained distant and enigmatic. I wanted to fall back and engage her in conversation, to gain her confidence, but the countess was like a limpet. I was her guest and her best friend for the evening.

The Opéra Garnier was, without doubt, the most opulent Baroque theatre I had ever had the good fortune to enter. My limited vocabulary cannot describe the feast of gold and marble that adorned the walls and ceilings of the grand stairway leading to the upper levels or the palatial communal areas.

Stewards ushered us into the grand foyer, where, despite my earlier efforts, I felt distinctly underdressed. Nothing short of a ballgown and a tiara would seem right in this setting. I half expected to play court to Louis XVI or Napoleon, though as Lawrence regaled us all as we toured the corridors, both were long dead when the theatre was built in the 1860s.

There were six red velvet chairs in the countess's box, arranged in three rows. Positioned to the left side of the stage overlooking the stalls, the first two seats had an incredible view.

Lawrence's height might allow him to see some of the stage, but I doubted anyone else behind Marta and me in the front row could watch anything. I offered to swap with Chloé, but she was busy with something on her phone and didn't answer me. I tried to attract her attention a second time, but Marta protested, and I had to acquiesce.

We had entered the box through a dark wooden door. Once we were all seated, Jeremy pulled a red curtain across the entrance, sealing us into a crimson and gold cave. I looked to the upper circle, and my grateful eyes rested upon the inspector. He had promised to fill the auditorium with police officers. If they were there, they were in plain clothes and blending in well with the paying public.

Lawrence leaned forward and whispered in my ear. "I hope this works."

I hope so too.

What exactly we hoped would work was a moot point. To say we had a plan would be an exaggeration. Basically, we had left the message for Anton and trusted he, or his accomplice, would make a play to take the memory stick during the performance.

We suspected someone sitting with us in this closed box might be the thief. Lawrence and I had hoped for further clues on the way to the theatre to avoid being blindsided by either suspect. I prayed for one of them to get an attack of the sniffles or something, but so far neither had given anything away.

Chloé's mood suggested to me she knew something was about to happen. If it all went wrong, who would she side with, her boss or her brother? How much of this skullduggery was she a willing participant in? Jeremy, on the other hand, pored over the theatre programme with Lawrence, combining their translation skills to share the narrative with the rest of us.

Men! They could have asked the Frenchwoman in the group!

The lights went out, and the auditorium buzzed with anticipation. A few polite 'ssshs' dampened the low-level humbug until silence reigned. The conductor's baton knocked three times, and orchestra strings filled the air. The curtain on stage parted, and a sea of dancers poured in from the wings. They wore leotards edged in matching chiffon skirts in shades of vibrant green and blue.

"They are representing the primordial ooze from which life sprung," whispered Jeremy from the back of the box.

Lawrence tapped my shoulder. "Many of them are wearing lime green, just like Marta's dress!"

Is this what I had seen after breakfast at the Café Vendôme? My premonition had been of the ballet? Were the dancers in danger? Surely not.

Fortunately, the first half continued without incident, and the ballerinas had changed outfits to reflect different stages of evolution. Part one ended with the dawn of humanity. It was all visually stunning, if not particularly profound.

As the curtain fell, there was a knock at the door. An usher in full livery handed in a note addressed to Lawrence. This was it! The game was on.

Lawrence made up some nonsense about his mother being ill and needing to make a phone call. Which Marta, at least, appeared to swallow hook, line and sinker. I made my apologies.

Obviously, I need to go with my soon-to-be fiancé in case it's bad news.

The note told Lawrence to head backstage. The usher who had passed on the message was waiting outside to guide the way. This was not at all what I expected from a thief who slashed cushions and trashed people's belongings. Someone more organised planned this. Someone who was very persuasive, or had the right contacts, or enough money. A bribe to the right people could open some useful doors.

The usher led us past the cast, all frantically changing for the second half, or snatching the opportunity to grab a drink or even a sneaky cigarette by the stage door. The usher scuttled along at a fair click. He tugged at the waistcoat of his livery constantly and kept his eyes rigidly in front as he walked. I hung back enough to text the inspector where we were, though as we walked deeper and deeper into the bowels of the theatre, I doubted he would find us.

We stopped in what looked like a basement with a hatch in the floor screened off from the public by metal railings.

"Wait here." The usher looked around and then dashed back the way we came.

"What do you think is under that hatch?" I was desperate to ease the tension as we waited.

"From pictures I've seen online, I'm guessing that's the entrance to the underground lake."

"As in *The Phantom of the Opera*?"

"Yes!" an eerily familiar male voice boomed across the empty space. "Seems apt on Halloween, don't you think?"

"Jeremy!"

"Yes, who were you expecting? Anton? That poor sap has messed this up too many times already." Jeremy emerged from the shadows and stopped under a blinking fluorescent light.

"As they say, if you want something done right, do it your-self. Though he came up trumps when he told me about this place. They used it for drills when he was a fireman. Most of the staff don't even know this is here." Jeremy laughed. "Your friend, the inspector, will never find us." He held out his hand expectantly. "Just hand it over, and we can go back to the show."

"What if we don't have it anymore?" I replied defiantly. "What if we've handed the memory stick over to the police already?"

Jeremy growled. "Well, that would be very stupid of you, now wouldn't it."

His forehead furrowed. The previously open hand went into his trouser pocket, from which he pulled out a black metal object. He flipped a button. The blade glinted under the white light as he lurched towards us.

Lawrence pushed me aside and grabbed our assailant's arm, bashing it down on the metal railings around the hatch. Jeremy's grip held firm. He thrust at Lawrence, who jumped back just enough to thwart the knife's path to his stomach.

I looked around for a weapon, but the room was bare. *Stilettos!* I yanked at the strap of my right shoe.

"AAAARGH!" I ran towards Jeremy, jumped onto his back, and beat him across the head with the sharp end of my four-inch heels.

He swatted me away like an annoying insect. I had inflicted minimal damage, but the distraction gave Lawrence time to grab the knife and turn the tables.

"Don't hurt him!"

We all turned to find Chloé in the doorway with the

inspector. Uniformed officers of the gendarmerie rushed from behind them, circling Lawrence and Jeremy, who threw their arms in the air. The inspector took the switchblade and bagged it for evidence.

"Arrest the American, and take the young lady as well." The police cuffed Jeremy and Chloé and led them away without protest.

"We caught the brother earlier. What is that term you use? He sang like a canary." The inspector thanked us both, said he could take our statements in the morning, and suggested we return to watch the rest of the show.

"I might need to get this seen to first." Lawrence raised his right arm. It was dripping with blood.

L'ÉPILOGUE

"It was so kind of the wardrobe mistress to dress your cut in some spare chiffon." I bit down into a welcome McDonald's Egg McMuffin.

"Yup, who'd have thought it was my blood you saw in your vision." Lawrence took a sip of coffee from a paper cup. "Lucky it was only a flesh wound. Just a couple of stitches. I'll soon be as right as rain."

"It was very gracious for Marta to pop by this morning. After all, we put her two closest staff members in prison. It must be like losing family."

"I think she had suspected they were up to something for a long time. So we were both right." Lawrence leaned back in his chair, folding his arms with great care. Only a slight wince ran across his face.

"Does it hurt much?"

"Just feels a little tender." He smiled. "I can't believe Chloé was Andy Warhol. I suppose she couldn't risk being recognised."

"And Jeremy sent in Anton when it went wrong because he thought Chloé was holding out on him. Using Anton meant the countess could give Jeremy and Chloé both an alibi. It would also throw suspicion elsewhere. Jeremy was the brains behind it. He put pressure on Chloé and her brother. Perhaps Anton was asking for money and when Jeremy learnt about him working at Bijoux, he hatched his plan. I would love to know what was on the *clé USB*."

"Very good, your French is improving." He laughed. "Customer account details or... I mean, they went to the American Embassy. Maybe they were selling state secrets?"

"Ah, no. I think that was to have lunch with the ambassador. It was completely unrelated."

"But your hunch? Did you make me take a taxi for nothing!"

"I told you, this stuff's hit or miss. Come on, drink up. We have a ferry to catch. I can't wait to get back home to Wesberrey. I have to relieve Reverend Cattermole. It's All Souls tomorrow, and he has two funerals booked."

"Of course. Just one thing before we go." Lawrence pushed back his chair and knelt down on one knee. He maintained his balance with one hand, whilst the other rummaged in his pocket. He pulled out a blue velvet box and, with a slight wobble, popped the lid open. Inside was a dazzling solitaire diamond ring.

"Jess, will you marry me?"

"You've just bought me McDonald's. How can I say no?"

The End

ABOUT THE AUTHOR

Penelope lives on an island off the coast of Kent, England, with her four children and an elderly Jack Russell Terrier. A lover of murder mystery and cups of tea (served with a stack of digestive biscuits), she writes quaint cosy mysteries and other feel-good stories from a corner table in the vintage tea shop on the high street. Penelope loves nostalgia and all things retro. Her taste in music is also very last century.

Find out more about Penelope at www.penelopecress.com.

WANT TO KNOW MORE?

Greenfield Press is the brainchild of bestselling author Steve Higgs. He specializes in writing fast paced adventurous mystery and urban fantasy with a humorous lilt. Having made his money publishing his own work, Steve went looking for a few 'special' authors whose work he believed in.

Georgia Wagner was the first of those, but to find out more and to be the first to hear about new releases and what is coming next, you can join the Facebook group by clicking the link below. Or copying the following link into your browser - www.facebook.com/GreenfieldPress

MORE BOOKS BY STEVE HIGGS - THE MISSING SAPPHIRE OF ZANGRABAR

When life gives you lemons, empty your cheating husband's bank accounts and go on a cruise.

That's right, isn't it?

Fuelled by anger, and decision impaired by gin, Patricia boards the world's finest luxury cruise ship for a three-month tour of the world …

… and awakes to find herself embroiled in a thirty-year-old priceless jewel theft.

Less than twenty-four hours after setting sail, she's accused of murder and confined to her cabin. Thankfully, she is staying in the royal suite and that means she has a butler to help her. When he recruits his gym instructor BFF, Barbie, the trio turn detective to find the real killer.

But someone on board doesn't want them to succeed and when the next body is found in her kitchen, the team realise it's more than just her freedom at stake.

They'd better solve this fast or all three of them might be next.

Read this fast-paced adventure as a middle-aged housewife throws off the shackles of her old life and becomes the woman she was always meant to be.

the mystery. He can already smell the answer – it's right before their noses.

He'll pitch in to help his human and the shop owner's teenage daughter as the trio set out to save the shop from closure. Is the rival pork pie shop across the street to blame? Or is there something far more sinister going on?

One thing is for sure, what started out as a bit of fun, is getting deadlier by the hour, and they'd better work out what the dog knows soon, or it could be curtains for them all.

FREE BOOKS AND MORE

Want to see what else I have written?

Go to my website -

https://stevehiggsbooks.com/

Or sign up to my newsletter where you will get sneak peaks, exclusive giveaways, behind the scenes content, and more. Plus, you'll be notified of Fan Pricing events when they occur and get exclusive offers from other authors because all UF writers are automatically friends.

Click the link or copy it carefully into your web browser. https://stevehiggsbooks.com/newsletter/

Prefer social media? Join my thriving Facebook community.

Want to join the inner circle where you can keep up to date with everything? This is a free group on Facebook where you can hang out with likeminded individuals and enjoy discussing my books. There is cake too (but only if you bring it).